PENELOPE OF THE "POLYANTHA"

BY
EDGAR WALLACE

British Library Cataloguing-in-Publication Data
A catalogue record for this book is available from
the British Library

EDGAR WALLACE

Richard Horatio Edgar Wallace was born in London, England in 1875. He received his early education at St. Peter's School and the Board School, but after a frenetic teens involving a rash engagement and frequently changing employment circumstances, Wallace went into the military. He served in the Royal West Kent Regiment in England and then as part of the Medical Staff Corps stationed in South Africa. However, Wallace disliked army life, finding it too physically testing. Eventually he managed to work his way into the press corps, becoming a war correspondent with the *Daily Mail* in 1898 during the Boer War. It was during this time that Wallace met Rudyard Kipling, a man he greatly admired.

In 1902, Wallace became editor of the *Rand Daily Mail*, earning a handsome salary. However, a dislike of "economising" and a lavish lifestyle saw him constantly in debt. Whilst in the Balkans covering the Russo-Japanese War, Wallace found the inspiration for *The Four Just Men*, published in 1905. This novel is now regarded as the prototype of modern thriller novels. However, by 1908, due to more terrible financial management, Wallace was penniless again, and he and his wife wound up living in a virtual slum in London. A lifeline came in the form of his *Sanders of the River* stories, serialized in a magazine of the day, which (despite being seen to contain pro-imperialist and racist overtones today) were highly popular, and sparked two decades of prolific output from Wallace.

Over the rest of his life, Wallace produced some 173 books and wrote 17 plays. These were largely adventure narratives with elements of crime or mystery, and usually combined a bombastic sensationalism with hammy violence. Arguably his best – and certainly his most successful, sparking as it did a semi-successful stint in Hollywood – work is his 1925 novel *The Gaunt Stranger*, later renamed *The Ringer* for the stage.

Wallace died suddenly in Beverly Hills, California in 1932, aged 57. At the time of his death, he had been earning what would today be considered a multi-million pound salary, yet incredibly, was hugely in debt, with no cash to his name. Sadly, he never got to see his most successful work – the 'gorilla picture' script he had earlier helped pen, which just a year after his death became the 1933 classic, *King Kong*.

NOVELS BY
EDGAR WALLACE

HODDER AND
STOUGHTON
Ltd., London

Contents

5

"THERE is a man in London—I guess he is still in London, though I have not had news of him in months—he'll be useful to you, Pen, if you ever need help."

Penelope Pitt dabbed her eyes savagely with the moist ball of linen that had once been a reputable and ladylike handkerchief, and tried to smile.

"I am a great fool, judge, blubbering like a baby. And I just hate Edmonton—and there is nobody here that I care a pin about. Besides, I shall never get to London. You'll find me working in a candy store at Moose Jaw."

"You've got your tickets for Toronto?" said the practical old man. "And Moose Jaw is a one-horse place—at least it was twenty years ago. Medicine Hat was worse.

7

Nelson is a live town. I wonder you don't make for the Kootnay. There are opportunities there. Why, a feller I knew——Here, take this letter, quick!"

The warning whistle had blown.

"Orford—James X. Orford; we were at school together in Berlin. They call it Kitchener since the war. And, Pen, you get through to me if you're held up in the East."

She kissed her hand to the white-haired figure on the platform as the train pulled out, the engine bell's clanging and the rattle and clash of wheels upon cross points drowning the sobs she tried heroically to stifle.

The great adventure had begun.

When she found her seat and had dried her eyes and told herself for the xth time how childish and weak she was to make such a sight of herself, Penelope discovered herself under the calm but inoffensive scrutiny of her *vis-à-vis*. She had already noticed and admired her, as much as she could notice or admire anything or anybody. Even old Judge Heron had interrupted his incoherent farewells to approve of the lady with the thin *spirituelle* face and the aristocratic carriage.

"Are you going far?"

The voice was soft and the strange lady had that drawling inflection which Pen associated with English women.

"To Toronto, I think," smiled Pen. "My plans aren't—yes, I think I am going to Toronto."

The woman nodded.

"You hate Edmonton, too? I detest the place. It is so raw and unfinished. You can almost smell the wood in the houses— and the hotels! They overcharge disgracefully."

Now Pen did not hate Edmonton at all. She loved it. Though she was born in England, Edmonton was her very home, and there was not stick or stone or brick of the city that she did not adore at this moment,

1*

when every puff from the big engine and every thump of the car wheels was carrying her away. She did not even hate the middle-aged merchant whose secretary she had been, though he had made violent love to her, and had offered to jettison his responsibilities (he had a daughter as old as she, and a large and pleasant wife) if she would run away with him. She certainly disliked the large and pleasant wife, who, in tidying her husband's desk, had discovered the draft of a letter which that optimistic man had written, believing that his suit would succeed. In this letter, he took farewell of his wife and family, outlined the material provisions he would make for their comfort, and quoted the Scriptures liberally. He was a churchwarden.

Upon Penelope, already distressed by the revelation of the effect which her grey eyes had had upon a bald-headed and Christian gentleman of no especial charm, swept the tornado of a woman scorned. She came through the interview a little dazed and feeling strangely unclean.

"No, I don't really hate Edmonton," she said quickly. "It is a dear town, only—well, I'm glad to get away."

"Are you thinking of taking a trip to England?"

Penelope laughed.

"That was one of my more extravagant ideas," she said, her lips twitching. "I might as well have planned a trip to the Pleiades."

The lady frowned.

"The——?"

"The stars," explained Pen.

Her companion nodded.

She was pretty. Pen had already decided that point. Her eyes were brown, sometimes they seemed almost black. She might have been twenty-eight—possibly she was less. Pretty, but—— Penelope saw the flaw. It was her mouth. It was too straight and the lips just a little too thin. Otherwise, she was beautiful. It was not Penelope's beauty—the beauty of the open. Pen was alive, vital. A creature of the prairies, tanned, clear skinned, straight backed. Pen was beautiful or nothing. "Pretty" was a term that could be applied only by those without a sense of word values.

The other woman was all prettiness. She belonged to the category of dainty china and fluffy kittens and all such expressions of the cute and the neat and the pleasing. Except her mouth : when she smiled, as she did quite readily, even that defect was scarcely noticeable.

Pen slept in the berth above her that night, and wondered who she was. She had to keep her mind upon matters that did not count, or she would have wept, for she was suffering an agony of loneliness. The steady thud of the wheels, which lulled her fellow-passengers to sleep, had the effect of making her wide awake. She went over and over her painful experience, neared the end of her mental narrative, and then switched quickly to the woman below, to the snoring sleepers, to the identity of the driver who was standing on the footplate of the engine—to anything.

She dozed at last, but, as it seemed, had scarcely slept before she woke again. Over the edge of her berth she saw the white face of her travelling companion.

Her brown eyes were staring roundly, her lip was trembling.

"Is anything wrong—are you ill?" asked Pen, sitting up.

The woman did not answer. She stood there, in the parting of the curtains, and stared blankly, her white hands gripping the edge of the berth.

Then, just as Penelope in her alarm was preparing to descend, she whispered, with a curious deliberation :

"Suppose he doesn't die? Have you thought of that, Arthur? Suppose he doesn't die, or Whiplow tells?"

She was asleep and yet awake. Instantly Pen had slipped from the berth and was at the woman's side.

She suffered herself to be put to bed again, and in a few minutes was breathing regularly.

Arranging her pillow, Pen disturbed a flat leather case which opened as she took it up. In the dim light of the berth she saw the portrait of an extremely good-looking young man. She wondered if this was "Arthur."

*   *   *   *   *

"Was I talking in my sleep—how fascinating. Do tell me what I said!"

Pen made the revelation in the dining-car at breakfast.

"Very little. I was so scared at seeing you, that I hardly know what you *did* say. You talked about somebody dying and you mentioned a name—Whiplow, was it?"

The woman was eyeing her gravely.

"No—I don't know that name. I've

never walked in my sleep before. I suppose I was a little overtired. Arthur? Oh
yes, of course. That was my husband. I
am Mrs. Arthur Dorban—Cynthia Dorban.
I thought I had told you last night. How
queer!"

Mrs. Dorban made no attempt to pursue
the subject and it was not mentioned again.
She said that she was going through to
Quebec after two days' stay in Toronto.
Pen gave confidence for confidence, so far
as her natural caution would allow her. She
did not mention the amorous stockbroker.

Mrs. Dorban received the girl's news
thoughtfully.

"You haven't a job to go to? And no
friends in Eastern Canada? What was it
I heard you telling the old gentleman? I
heard almost every word you said. Are you
really going to England?"

Pen shook her head laughingly.

" That was a mad scheme of mine—one of
my very unsubstantial dreams. I want to

go. I was born in London. I've always had a longing to see Europe—but, of course, I shall never be able to afford the trip."

There was a long silence. The train was rushing through a boundless ocean of waving wheat. As far as the eye could reach, the yellow waves billowed and swayed—from horizon to horizon there was no sign of human habitation. Nothing but this waste of billowing yellow.

"Do you get the English newspapers at Edmonton? Naturally they come to you, but do you read them?"

Penelope shook her head.

"I am afraid I am not a very close student of English affairs," she confessed. "I know that Mr. Lloyd George is Prime Minister, and that there is trouble with Ireland, but——"

Mrs. Dorban changed the subject. She talked for a while about her home in Devonshire, her cliff garden, a wilderness of gorse and pine that sloped steeply up to the edge of Borcombe Downs. Once she made a casual reference to a name that had a familiar sound.

"Lord Rivertor? Oh yes, he has a ranch near our farm—that is, the farm my father had before he came into Edmonton. I lived there most of my life. I never saw him— Lord Rivertor I mean. He died last year, didn't he?"

"Yes."

Mrs. Dorban appeared to have lost interest in the deceased Earl of Rivertor, for she went off at a tangent to the value of farm lands in the West, a subject on which Penelope was something of an authority, since her late employer had speculated successfully in land and it had been her business to keep a record of his transactions.

Two days later, when the train was within an hour of Toronto, Cynthia Dorban made her astounding and delightful proposal.

Penelope listened open-mouthed, hardly daring to believe her ears.

"But—how wonderful! Do you think Mr. Dorban will agree?"

"He has already agreed," said Cynthia Dorban with a little smile. "I cabled him from Winnipeg and had the answer on the train at Fort William. He thinks it is an excellent suggestion. He doesn't like English secretaries. There is the job, Penelope—you don't mind if I call you Penelope? You can call me Cynthia; I should prefer it. It will be very uninteresting, because at the moment we are buried away in the country——"

"You've taken my breath away—I jump at the offer! It is a dream come true!"

The Empire Express was slowing into Toronto before Penelope had realized that she had engaged herself to leave for England in forty-eight hours.

PENELOPE had gone to the railway station to make reservations for the following day's boat train to Quebec. It was only a "boat train" in the sense that it connected with the C.P.R. steamer that left a few hours after the train's arrival in the capital city, but to Penelope it enjoyed the dignity and importance of a special run for her alone and labelled from smoke stack to rear light "Penelope Pitt's European Special."

The New York express had just come in as she entered the booking-hall, and she watched with enjoyable awe the privileged folk who had travelled from that mysterious city and who now strode toward the exits with the utmost nonchalance, as though it was nothing very remarkable to have lived in and journeyed from that wonder-place.

At last the stream thinned, and with a sigh she turned to the business which had brought her to the depôt. She had taken the tickets and was walking slowly toward the big exit when a man smiled at her. Before she realized her indiscretion, she had smiled back at him. He was tall and fair, and when he raised his hat she saw that he was slightly bald. Evidently he had just arrived by the express, for his grip and a light dust coat were at his feet, and he had the slightly soiled appearance of a careless traveller.

To do her justice she thought that she knew him—it might have been somebody she had met in Edmonton; her employer had many business associates and it was not unlikely that this was one.

"Good-afternoon! Met you somewhere, eh? Detroit. No? St. Paul, maybe. Met a lot of people in St. Paul."

"I'm afraid we are both mistaken," she said, and would have passed on, but with a quick glance round to see if he was under the scrutiny of an unsympathetic official he intercepted her.

"Don't go, little girl. You can't know how glad I am to meet a real Canadian. I'm British. Where's the best place in this burg to get a good cup of tea? That's English, eh?" he chuckled throatily.

"I am not well acquainted with Toronto," she said. "One of the porters will tell you."

"What's the hurry?" he demanded truculently. "You talked to me first, didn't you? Laughed at me, didn't you?"

She walked quickly past him, but, grabbing his suitcase, he followed and overtook her before she was clear of the building.

"What's the hurry, huh? Not offended, are you, little lady? I'd like to know you. My name's Whiplow——"

She stopped, staring at him.

Whiplow? She remembered the name instantly. It was that which Mrs. Dorban had spoken in her sleep. A coincidence? It was not a very common name.

"Johnny Whiplow. What's yours?"

"You had best ask Mrs. Dorban," she said.

It was a shot at a venture, but the effect upon the man was amazing. The colour went from his cheeks, leaving his face the colour of putty, his prominent eyes seemed to start from their sockets.

"M - Mrs. Dorban?" he squeaked. "Here—she's not here——"

But, making good use of his confusion, she escaped, and by the time Mr. Whiplow had reached the street the girl had disappeared.

She did not mention her meeting to Mrs. Dorban; in the twenty-four hours they were in Toronto she did not see her employer for longer than a quarter of an hour at a time, and only when they had boarded the train and were flying eastward to Quebec did she speak of her experience.

"Whiplow—you are sure? What was he like? Yes, that was he. The brute! That was always his weakness, a pretty face. He is the type of man who haunts the streets where shop girls pass on their way to work. But in Toronto?"

She bit her lip and frowned at the fields that were flying past. Then:

"I thought he was in South America. What can he be doing in Canada? Humph!"

Her delicate face grew hard, and her eyes narrowed.

"He said nothing after you had told him that you knew me? Was it necessary to tell him? I suppose it was. In fact, I am glad you did. Otherwise, I should not have been certain it was he."

Then in her abrupt way she switched the talk to such mundane matters as what trunk Pen had put her writing-case in—Pen had assisted in her packing. As they were boarding the ship she thought she saw Whiplow standing on the upper deck, one of a group of passengers that were leaning over the rail.

When she looked again the man had disappeared, and she was not to see him again throughout the voyage.

She felt more than a little homesick as the land fell away, but overcame this childish emotion (so she described it) with no great effort. The life on board ship was so delightfully novel: the ship had in itself the elements of romance, and the future gave her so much food for thought that within two days of sailing Canada and the life she had left seemed almost like a dream.

Cynthia spoke very little about her husband, and only then when the girl raised the subject. Pen did not think it remarkable that Mrs. Dorban should have gone all the way to Canada to secure a secretary, when thousands of capable women were available in England. She regarded her engagement as an act of freakish generosity on Cynthia's part, and had a warm and grateful feeling toward her.

One day, tidying the woman's cabin—and

Cynthia, despite her precise and business-like way, was an extremely untidy person—she came across a sheet of paper. Scribbled across its face in pencil was what was evidently the draft of a cable. It was addressed : "Dorban, Stone House, Borcombe, England," and ran : "Got the right kind of girl for secretary; insist on your discharging Willis. Probably she has been sent by Stamford Mills. This girl knows nothing of case, has no friends in England."

Penelope was momentarily perturbed. She had not the slightest doubt that the cablegram referred to her. Who was Stamford Mills, and what was the case to which Mrs. Dorban referred? She felt uncomfortable, apprehensive. There were two or three sentences in the draft that had been struck out, and she attempted to decipher them. One undoubtedly was : "She is not the kind who would talk."

Penelope folded the paper and put it away. For the first time since the adventure began she felt doubtful of her wisdom. And yet there might be, and probably was, a very simple explanation of this mysterious message.

At the earliest opportunity she turned the conversation in the direction of Mr. Dorban.

"My husband hates towns," said Cynthia languidly. She was reclining in her chair on the upper deck, and appeared loath to discuss her partner or his business. "We are very quiet people; Arthur is a student and seldom goes anywhere. I hope you are prepared for a very dull time, Penelope?"

Penelope laughed.

"I feel that a dull time is just what I need," she said.

"You will get all you want," replied Cynthia a little grimly. "We have no visitors and no dances or dinner parties, and unless you are keen on fishing——" She hesitated. "Perhaps later you will have a much better time than you imagine," she said. "The only thing I would impress upon you, Penelope—you don't mind me calling you by your Christian name, do you? I told you to call me Cynthia if you wished; I hate 'Mrs. Dorban.' What was I saying? Oh yes, later you will have a much better time—— No, it wasn't that. There is one thing I want to impress upon you, Penelope, and that is that we shall rely upon you to maintain the strictest confidence as to my husband's business. Not that he has any business, you understand?"

Penelope did not understand, but she nodded.

"But there is a whole lot of research work to be done, particulars of estates to be put in order—my husband has great expectations. We hope some day to inherit a very large fortune." She looked round and lowered her voice, leaning slightly over the edge of her chair. "There is another point upon which I want to warn you. My husband has a very bitter enemy, a man who has tried over and over again to ruin him. I don't know the reason," said Mrs. Dorban with a calmness which, under the circumstances, seemed to Penelope a little unearthly, "but I fancy there is a woman in it. I don't want to know the truth, but the cause is neither here nor there. Stamford Mills is always sending spies to pry into our affairs. Who is he? I don't quite know. He is a man about town. A person who lives by his wits. Some say he is a swindler, but I don't wish to slander the man. All that I do know is that he is an implacable enemy of ours, and it is only right that you should be warned against him."

"But what does he expect to discover— I mean, when he sends people to investigate your affairs?" asked Penelope, troubled.

"God knows," said Mrs. Dorban piously. "Hand me my book, Penelope. I wish this beastly ship didn't roll so."

The rolling of the ship in no way inconvenienced Penelope Pitt. She might have been born upon the ocean, so little did the motion affect her. She loved to sit upon the deck and watch the mile-wide trough of the green seas, to feel beneath her the shiver and shudder of the racing turbines, or to stand by the fore-rail and take the sting of the breeze to her cheeks.

The passengers did not greatly interest her. Her chief source of recreation was the deck steward, an apple-faced man, who took her under his charge from the day they left Quebec. In slack times, generally in the early part of the afternoon when the passengers were dozing in their bunks, and the deck, particularly on dull days, was deserted, he would stand by her chair and unburden himself of endless and fascinating reminiscences of the sea and ships and the people who travelled in ships. Once he had been a smoke-room steward, he told her with some pride, on a big Western ocean liner, and travelled between New York and Southampton, and it was on the subject of his experi-

ences at this period of his life that he was
most interesting.

Beddle (this was his name) had met with
many bad men, and he could talk for hours
upon the gangs that went backward and
forward across the ocean all the year round,
living by the dexterity of their delicate hands.

"I knew 'em all, Lew Marks, Billy
Sanders, Jimmy the Hook, Long Charlie,
Denver John—— Lord, I could go on for
hours, and give you a list as long as your
arm, miss!"

"Were they all card-sharpers?" she asked.

He nodded.

"But the worst of 'em was El Slico—
some American girl gave him that name and
it stuck. He was that slick and smart. I've
never seen El Slico in the same suit twice.
His kit must have cost him a fortune, and
he always travelled in the best suite, not like
some of the gangs that go four to a cabin.
Quite a young fellow, too—at least he was
in my days, and that's only a few years ago

—and according to what I heard very highly connected. But what a villain! He would take the gold filling out of your teeth, if there was nothing else to take. He was one of a gang that worked the high-class people. And what a brain! El Slico never depended on chance meetings aboard ship. There was a man from Colorado that he soaked for a hundred and fifty thousand dollars, a hardware millionaire. Slico knew he was coming to Europe, and went to Colorado to meet him a fortnight before the ship sailed; got to know him at his club, was invited to his house to dinner, all the time pretending that he was a rich young Englishman, with nothing to do in life but to burn money. Naturally, when they met on board the ship they were big friends—it cost Mr. Gifford a hundred and fifty thousand dollars, and even then he didn't know that El Slico was the head of the gang that made the killing."

Day after day Penelope heard stories of the redoubtable Mr. Slico, a favourite

character of Mr. Beddle's. Sometimes it was
of a too confident passenger who had been
induced to join a select bridge party, sometimes of a private exploit, sometimes of a
vendetta pursued by the Slico gang against
some other band of miscreants which had
queered the other's operations; and always
the story redounded to the discredit of this
prince of sharpers.

From the experienced traveller's point of
view, the voyage was wholly uninteresting.
The ship steamed within view of three ice-
bergs, sighted innumerable other ships; there
was a dance, a fancy dress ball, a concert
in the saloon, and the inevitable Sunday
service, all of which were fascinating to the
girl from Edmonton.

It was when they were one day out of
Liverpool, and had passed the low-lying grey
blur on the ocean which somebody told her
was Ireland, that Penelope had her first
revelation of one side of Mrs. Dorban's
character which she had never suspected.

Cynthia had a little toy Pomeranian. She had bought it in Winnipeg and was devoted to the fluffy little beast. It was seldom out of her arms in the daytime, and slept at the foot of her bed at night.

Pen was a dog lover, but she loved them big. These little morsels of life that women petted and combed and brushed and carried as they would carry a vanity case made no appeal to her. She was sorry for them.

The ship was swinging into the Mersey, and Pen was standing on the promenade deck watching with kindling eyes the unromantic shores of Lancashire looming through a sea mist, when Cynthia joined her, and the first thing that Pen noticed was that the dog was no longer in her arms.

"Where is Fluff, Mrs. Dorban?" she asked.

"Poor little beast," said Cynthia regretfully. "And such a nice little dog, too."

"What has happened?" asked the girl in surprise.

2

" They told me I shouldn't be able to take it ashore, and it would have to go into quarantine. I really can't be bothered with quarantine. Dogs catch all sorts of queer diseases, so I gave him to a sailor and told him to drown him. He wanted me to let him keep it and take a chance of smuggling it ashore, but I wasn't going to pay a hundred and fifty dollars for a dog to give to a sailor," said Cynthia; " so I made him swear he would tie something to the poor little beggar's neck and throw him overboard."

Penelope gasped.

" But," she stammered, " I thought you were so fond of him."

" I like him all right," said Cynthia carelessly. " He's a dear little fellow, but I don't think he is as well bred as that person in Winnipeg told me. That tall Colonel Wilkins, who knows a great deal about dogs, said that he was not a thoroughbred, and that I had been imposed upon. Of course, my dear, I can't be bothered with half-bred dogs. Are you packed?"

Penelope could say nothing. The calm callousness of the woman shocked her. It was not a very big thing; the life of one pet Pomeranian did not mean much to Penelope, but it almost hurt her to discover this trait in the character of one of whom she was not inordinately fond, but whom, in an abstract way, she admired. Those thin lips of hers! Penelope looked at them with a new interest and wonder.

A few privileged friends of the passengers came out on a tug, and Cynthia casually mentioned the possibility that her husband might be amongst them. She showed, however, no sign of pleasurable excitement at the prospect of the reunion, and did not even trouble to join the fringe of people that were looking over the side as the tug transferred its passengers.

Penelope had packed both her own and

Cynthia's belongings, and now went in search of her deck steward.

"Thank you, miss," said Beddle, as he took the five-dollar note from the girl's hand. "You needn't have given me this—it has been a pleasure—thank you all the same, miss. I suppose we shall be seeing you again. Are you on a holiday visit, miss?"

"I hope it will be a holiday," smiled the girl, "but in reality I have come over to work."

The apple-faced man rubbed his chin thoughtfully.

"It is not a bad country. Great Moses!"

She saw his eyes travel past her, and his jaw drop, and then he grinned slowly.

"Quick, miss," he hissed. "That's him!"

"Him—who?" Penelope turned her head in the direction he was looking. She saw a smart, clean-shaven man, immaculately attired from his polished silk hat to his lemon-coloured gloves. He seemed an incongruous figure on board ship, a tailor's mannequin that had been lifted from Bond Street and transported without crease or injury to the atmosphere of the sea.

His face was sallow and dark, his black moustache was small and tidy. His jaw was a little long, and he was, at the moment, smiling, showing two regular rows of white teeth.

" El Slico !" whispered Beddle, and then, before the girl could take him in, Cynthia came hurrying toward her.

" Penelope dear," she said, " I want to introduce you." She took the girl's arm and hurried her toward the sallow-faced exquisite. " I want you to meet my husband, Mr. Dorban," said Cynthia.

" El Slico " lifted his hat from his glossy head, and extended a thin, long hand.

Penelope took it mechanically.

THE deck steward must have been mistaken, Penelope told herself a thousand times on the journey between Liverpool and London. Of course it was absurd, ridiculous, to suggest that this pleasant man was the head of an infamous gang that preyed upon the foolish. And it was so easy to make a mistake. Mr. Dorban's type was not an unusual one. Of course it was absurd. Why should a card-sharper want a secretary? Why should he be living in retirement in a Devonshire village, a man of great expectations, of so many business activities that he needed secretarial help?

The greeting between husband and wife had been a perfunctory one; neither seemed especially overjoyed at meeting the other. Mr. Dorban had reserved a compartment and they were alone. Once Penelope wondered whether she should not stroll out into the corridor and allow them to talk by themselves, but at the very first hint of her intentions, Cynthia stopped her.

Mr. Dorban himself was an interesting companion. It seemed to the girl that he talked all the time from the moment the train drew out from the riverside station until it pulled into Euston. His voice was soft and well modulated, his humour subtle, the stories he told excellent.

He had brown eyes, and ordinarily Penelope did not like men with brown eyes, but she thought she could like Mr. Arthur Dorban. Indeed, she felt more at home with him than she had with Cynthia. He knew Canada slightly.

"I have been there once, when I was young, but I hate the sea," he said. "I would sooner lose ten thousand than cross the Atlantic again.

"Have you crossed many times?" asked the girl curiously.

"Twice," said Arthur Dorban, with a twinkle in his eye. "If I hadn't crossed it twice, I shouldn't have been here, Miss Pitt!"

They spent the night at the Station Hotel in Paddington. Mrs. Dorban hired a car and drove the girl through the Park, and Penelope was amazed and delighted. She had always pictured London as a huddle of squat, dingy brick houses; she was delighted with the Park, with the background of towers and steeples that showed behind the dusky green of the trees, with the silvery stretch of lake, with the multifarious colouring of the flowers, and the noble vista of the Mall.

They left the next morning by an early train for Torquay, and reached Borcombe in time for a late lunch.

Stone House stood on a fold of the green downs at the seaward edge of Borcombe village. A rambling house, invisible from the red cliffs above, and half hidden by the belt of sycamores from the beach below, it had been built at the end of the eighteenth century by a recluse who, for his own private reason, desired isolation from the world.

The house was approached by a steep narrow road that wound down the face of the cliff, and its consequent inaccessibility had been a grievance to generations of tradesmen.

To Pen it was a paradise. The sloping garden was a kaleidoscopic tangle of flowers, wild and cultivated. At the lower end of the garden, hidden by a continuous hedge of lilac, was a brick wall pierced by one ancient door which led to a private path (it was less of a path than a series of stone steps terminating in a broad, weather-worn rock) to the shed where Mr. Dorban's stout motor-boat was moored. The span of the shed ran between two flat rocks, and Nature had thus created an ideal quay, for the boathouse was sited in the hollow of a tiny bay, and was protected from stormy seas by two short reefs

2*

that jutted straightly into the sea, forming a natural breakwater.

"Delightful, isn't it?" said Cynthia mechanically.

It seemed that her interest in such things was invariably mechanical. Her mind was so completely occupied by the practical things of life, the bread and the butter of it.

"Yes. It is a long way from the village, but I have a car which saves the climb. Can you drive?"

Penelope nodded.

"Now you had better see your room," said Cynthia, and led the way up a broad flight of stairs, down a long and dark passage, to a room at the end.

It was small and simply furnished, but it had two windows which looked out upon the emerald and amethystine sea, upon the red cliffs and the green fields atop.

She drew a deep breath.

"Do you like it?" asked Cynthia, watching her closely.

"It is lovely," she breathed.

Mrs. Dorban laughed shortly.

"It is my idea of hell," she said.

*   *   *   *   *

The days passed with amazing rapidity. Penelope found that there was much more work than she had anticipated. A room on the ground floor had been set apart as a study, and generally she occupied this alone.

After breakfast, taken in the panelled low-ceilinged dining-room, she went to the study, and from then until lunch-time she was engaged in an examination of leases and other documents pertaining to estates in various parts of the country.

She noticed that they were not original documents, being for the main part certified copies which had apparently been secured by a legal agency in London. Her task was to reduce to an understandable and tabulated form the cash values of the properties to which they referred. For her guidance she had innumerable sale catalogues, reports of auctions, returns of land values.

"Of course, I can't expect you to get the exact value of every one of these properties," said Mr. Dorban the first morning she began her work, "and it is going to be a devil of a job to get even the approximate value, but prices are fairly steady, and what one farm will fetch in Norfolk is roughly the value of another."

To assist her further, the estate pages of *The Times* and other newspapers were sent to her from day to day. The remainder of the newspapers she never saw. Indeed, all the time she was at Stone House, a newspaper never came her way.

She found it a little difficult to reconcile Cynthia's description of her husband as a student with facts as she discovered them. There were not twenty books in the house. Cynthia was a subscriber to a local library, and there was generally a supply of the latest novels, which neither she nor her husband ever read; Pen had an idea that the subscription to the library was taken out solely on her own account, and in this she was not mistaken. She never spoke to the servants, for the excellent reason that she could not speak their language, for all the domestics of the house, except the gardener, were French, in which language Penelope was indifferently proficient.

The afternoons and the evenings were her own, and yet not her own. She was never allowed out to go to the village alone : either Cynthia or Mr. Dorban accompanied her. Sometimes he would drive her about the country, sometimes the three would go out for a sea trip on the *Princess*, his motor-boat. She had the uncomfortable sensation that she was being guarded, and this she resented.

And then a new, and perhaps inevitable, complication appeared.

One day when Cynthia had gone to London on business she was working in her study when Mr. Dorban walked in. He was, as usual, spick and span.

"Leave those wretched things and come fishing," he said.

Penelope hesitated. His attitude towards her had been scrupulously correct. She made some excuse, which he overrode.

"Nonsense," he said. "That can wait till to-morrow. You have two years to get those beastly papers in order."

"I often wonder why you did not do all this work yourself," she said, as they made their way down the steep steps to the beach. "It is not really very difficult, and you know so much more about the subject than I."

He was whistling softly to himself, a characteristic of his, and he did not answer, for some time, until they had reached the boathouse.

"I hate figures," he said. "I hate office work of any kind. God made me for the free and open spaces of the world, for the sea——"

"I thought you disliked the sea."

"I dislike big ships; I dislike long voyages," he answered briefly, and changed the subject.

The boat chugged out into the placid waters of Borcombe Bay, Penelope steering, the fastidious Mr. Dorban, who had covered himself with a white overall, attending to the powerful engines.

They were three miles from shore when he stopped the engine and sat down.

"Well, what do you think of England?" he asked.

"Aren't you going to fish?"

He shook his head.

"I have brought no lines," he said simply. "Fishing bores me. Come for'ard."

The forepart of the boat was comfortably upholstered, and there was a small folding table, which was now extended.

Again she hesitated. She had a feeling that something unpleasant was going to happen, and she wished she had not come.

Mr. Dorban was crouched up over the table, and in his thin hand was a pack of cards, which he shuffled mechanically. His melancholy brown eyes were gazing shoreward, and his thin lips were down-turned as though, of a sudden, a weight of a great sorrow had fallen upon him. The change was so remarkable that she looked at him fascinated, and then suddenly he turned and looked at her.

"What do you think of Cynthia?" he asked surprisingly.

"What a curious question!" Penelope forced a smile.

"It isn't curious; it is very natural," he said. "Look, I will show you a trick. Shuffle those cards."

He pushed the pack toward her, and she took it.

"Shuffle," he said almost impatiently, and she obeyed.

"Cynthia is rather a cold-blooded mortal," he said. "I suppose that fact has struck you. She is a mind, and minds are rather trying things to live with."

"Here are your cards," said Penelope.

He took the pack in his slender hands, and for a moment the edges were a blur of white and gold, then he began to deal them face upwards. Ace, king, queen, jack, and so through the whole sequence of diamonds. Suit by suit he dealt, each card placed according to its value, and she looked open-mouthed, for she had shuffled the pack thoroughly, and here he was dealing them as though they had been carefully arranged by her in order.

El Slico! The deck steward's words came back to her.

"Well?" He was smiling.

"How did you do it?" she gasped. "I'm sure I shuffled them." In her interest she forgot her apprehension.

"Shuffle them again," he said.

Again she shuffled, deliberately sorting out the cards so that no two suits were together, and again taking the pack from her hand, he dealt the suits in order.

" That's the most wonderful trick I have ever seen."

" Is it?" he asked carelessly, and slipped the cards into his pocket. " What do you think of Cynthia?" he asked again.

" That is hardly a question I expected you to ask," said Penelope. " She has been most kind to me."

" Cynthia is kind to nobody," said Arthur Dorban promptly. " I sometimes wish that Cynthia was dead." He said this so quietly that she could hardly believe her ears.

" Mr. Dorban!" she said, shocked, and he laughed.

" You think I'm a brute, but I'm not really," he said. " I know of no other way of getting rid of Cynthia except by her dying. By that look on your face I gather that you are thinking I am contemplating an extensive use of weed-killer, which is so

popular in these parts. As a matter of fact,
I am not; I am merely stating an unpalat-
able truth. There is no way of getting rid of
Cynthia. I have discussed the matter with
her, you will be interested to know, and she
has agreed that she is immovable. I can't
divorce her, and she would not divorce me.
I can't run away from her, for reasons which
I will not at the moment discuss; I cannot
ill-treat her, because it is not my nature to
ill-treat women, and the very idea is repugnant to my finest feelings; and I cannot even
get her certified as insane, because she is the
least mad person I know. And yet," he went
on without pause, "my very soul aches for
sympathetic companionship, for the love
which Cynthia has never shown—Cynthia
and I are only married in the legal sense—
for the warmth and blind devotion of which
Cynthia is wholly incapable."

She could only listen in dumbfounded
silence.

"Cynthia knows this, of course. I think she chose you because she thought that you would keep me soothed."

"Do you know what you are saying, Mr. Dorban?" said Penelope sternly.

"I know exactly what I am saying," said Mr. Dorban, and slowly rolled a cigarette. "I am asking you to love me."

Penelope rose and went back to the after-way of the boat, and he followed her.

"We will go home now, I think, and since you have rejected my discreditable advances, we will not discuss the matter any more, and you may forget that I have ever spoken on the subject. If you do not trust me, and you wish to go back to Canada, I will see that you will have your fare to-morrow, in spite of Cynthia's protests. If, on the other hand, you will take my word, and the word of El Slico——"

"El Slico!" Her mouth opened in amazement, and he chuckled softly.

"Of course, you knew I was El Slico. I

saw you talking to old Beddle, who knows me quite well. And old Beddle recognized me and told you who I was. Yes, I am El Slico, but you needn't mention the fact to Cynthia, who would have a thousand fits if she thought I had been recognized."

"But, Mr. Dorban," said the bewildered girl, "you can't expect me to stay."

"You may stay or go, as you wish," said Arthur Dorban, starting the engine. "I strongly advise you to stay. In justice to me you will admit that I have been very frank, and that my methods have been transparently honest. I don't think I should go back to Canada if I were you. You may please yourself as to whether you tell Cynthia—she will probably guess. I don't think she will respect you any more for your virtues."

She did not make any reply to this, and spent the rest of the afternoon in her room. It was a grotesque situation, and if it had happened in Canada she might have dealt with the position sanely. As it was, she was

in a strange land, friendless and alone.
Somehow she was impressed by the man's
candour. She did not know that the principal weapon in El Slico's armoury was his
engaging frankness. Should she take him
at his word and leave, or should she stay
on until she had saved a sufficient sum to
enable her to take the chance of seeking her
fortune in London? Rightly or wrongly,
Penelope decided to stay, and remembered,
as she fell asleep, that somewhere in London
was Mr. James Orford, to whom she might
turn in a moment of crisis.

SHE 'was down early the next morning, and went into the garden to work again round the circle of her problem.

It was six o'clock. The mist which had laid on the sea all night had lifted, and the opalescent stretch of Borcombe Bay was set with a million flashing points.

She sat on a rustic bench taking in the soft and lovely colouring of the scene. The deep red of the Devonshire cliffs, the white of the distant beaches, the rich green of the fields that ran to the cliff's edge, a glimpse of a primrose road that dipped out of sight toward Teignmouth—these she saw over the uneven edge of a great bank of moss roses that charged the morning air with heavy fragrance.

The colour of it—— She held her breath

and for a while forgot her difficulties and worries. Beyond the late lilac was a tumbled wilderness of golden gorse; to the left she saw the spire of the Church of St. Mary's, just the grey tip of it showing above the houses on the cliff head. The house was approached by a steep and crooked drive. From where she sat she could not see the gates, but in the still morning air the " clack " of the catch sounded almost as though the gate were near at hand. She looked up, curious to discover who their early visitor might be. At first she did not recognize him in his grey suit and straw hat. Evidently he did not see her, for he advanced toward the house with a certain caution that suggested a doubt as to his welcome.

Avoiding the gravelled paths, he walked upon the grass that bordered the flower-beds and he came very slowly, his eyes upon the upper windows. Then with a start he saw her, hesitated a second, and came toward her.

"Good-morning, miss." He spoke in a low voice as if he did not wish to be overheard.

"Good-morning."

Mr. Whiplow looked round again at the house with a little grimace.

"Mrs. Dorban about? I suppose you told her you met me? Didn't see me on the ship, eh? I'll bet you didn't!"

"Mrs. Dorban has gone to London—do you wish to see Mr. Dorban?" she asked coldly.

"Yeh. I can deal with Arthur. He's got sense, that boy. But she——!" He peered forward at her, his fishlike eyes searching her face keenly. "She hasn't told you anything?" He jerked his thumb toward the house. "Don't kid me that she has an' try to pump me. I know she 'asn't." He was a little careless of his aspirates. "Funny thing meeting you in Toronto—coincidence —only shows you how small the world is. Don't go!"

"I will send one of the servants up to tell Mr. Dorban," she began, when the appearance of Arthur Dorban in the open doorway of the house made any further action unnecessary.

Mr. Dorban was fully dressed, and under his arm he carried a gun. It was perfectly understandable to Penelope that he should be so armed, for the little estate was overrun with rabbits, and sometimes he would spend the whole morning roaming about on a mission of extermination. But to Mr. Whiplow the appearance of that weapon had an especial significance. His face was distorted in a grimace of fear, and his jaw dropped. Then with remarkable celerity he jumped behind Pen and spoke shrilly over her shoulder.

"None of that, Arthur! You put that gun down, see?"

Mr. Dorban's white teeth showed in a smile of amusement. With a jerk he threw open the breech of the gun.

"Not loaded, Whip. Come away from
that lady; you're scaring her."

He put the gun down and advanced
toward them, hands in pockets. Whiplow's
eyes never left him.

"You came over in the same boat as my
wife?" said Arthur. "Where have you
been?"

"In the country," said Whiplow emphatically. "I wouldn't have come, Slic—Arthur,
I mean—only I was fed with America."

"You might have written; we would have
had the best guest-room prepared, and hired
the village band to meet you at the station."

El Slico's gentle irony veiled something
that was not so gentle.

"You know Miss Pitt, of course; you
tried to make an impression upon her.
What a lady-killer you are, Whip!"

Whiplow licked his lips and said nothing.

"You will excuse us?" Dorban's question-
ing eyebrows rose, and she inclined her head

slowly. She felt rather unnecessary. When they had gone out of sight into the house, she returned to her bench and a new angle of speculation. "Whiplow will tell!" She remembered the words whispered to her over the edge of the sleeping-berth. Tell what? Tell whom? Was Arthur Dorban hiding from the consequence of some crime? That was very unlikely. He was well-known in the village, and patrolling policemen passed the time of day with him. He made no attempt to hide himself.

She was annoyed with her own stupidity, that some perfectly simple solution of this queer situation did not immediately present itself. Men, and women too, did queer things that they did not wish should be exposed. Not necessarily criminal things—unpleasant, unsavoury things not to be talked about and to be tactfully forgotten. Somehow, she knew that the question of El Slico's shady record had nothing to do with the need for Whiplow's silence. It was another matter altogether.

She sighed and got up. Out at sea she saw the black outline of a ship that seemed to be traversing the farthermost edge of the ocean. Hearing a sound, she turned her head. It was the Dorban's gardener, their one English servant.

"Mornin', miss. Looking at the *Polyantha?*"

"*Poly*—you mean that ship? Do you know her?"

"Ay. She were in Tor Bay last night an' I seed her. Belongs to a French gentleman, so 'tis said. Her's been takin' in stores by Dartmouth."

"Is she a passenger ship?"

The gardener's mouth slewed sideways in amusement.

"Her's a yat."

"A——? Oh, a yacht! She's a very big yacht."

The gardener, who by birth and training was unwilling to admit superiority of any foreign ship, thought there were larger. He wouldn't swear to it, but he thought. . . .

She made her escape from the loquacious man and left him snail-hunting. Arthur Dorban and his visitor were in the drawing-room. She heard Arthur's hard voice distinctly. For want of something better she went into the library. Later she saw the two men pacing the garden path on that side of the house. Arthur's quick eyes missed nothing visible, observed the figure by the desk, and led his companion out of sight.

"Whiplow," he said for the third time, "you're the first man in this world who has ever double-crossed me and got away with it."

"You've said that before," growled Whiplow. "And how have I double-crossed you, Arthur? I can't stand America; it's too serious for a man like me, used to life and jollity. My God! You've no idea how serious they are! If you happen to mention butter at breakfast in a boarding-house, there's three people at the table who'll give you a lecture on butter 't'll last all morning. There's another thing. They don't say 'all the morning,' they say 'all morning'; and they don't say 'I haven't seen him for a month,' they say 'in a month.' It rattles me."

"That seems a pretty good excuse for breaking your solemn oath, you poor herring!" snarled Dorban, his brown eyes gleaming. "The sensitive ear and the joyous soul of a damned Cockney thief!"

"Easy!" murmured the other.

He himself was not easy.

"You came back because you went gambling in Mexico and lost your money—money that should have lasted you out for two years. And you've come back to sponge —but, Whip, I'm dry. You'll get enough from me to keep you on the lower scale, and it will be paid you weekly. And if you look like squealing—just *look* like it—I'll quieten you. Get that!"

Mr. Whiplow wriggled uncomfortably.

"I've got to live," he pleaded. "Now haven't I got to live, Arthur?"

"I hope so," said Arthur Dorban significantly, and his guest turned pale.

"We'll talk it over. I'll have the girl sent to town. Go up to the village and take a wire to Cynthia."

At eleven o'clock came a telegram from Mrs. Dorban, saying: "Send Penelope to town by midday train. I will meet her at Paddington."

Penelope went gratefully, and with deliberate intention slipped past the waiting Cynthia and made her way out of the station by the subway.

MR. JAMES XENOCRATES ORFORD admitted frankly and without reservation that it was hot. Hitherto it had been a case of "Hot? Say, do you call this hot? Why, over in New York they'd have all the radiators goin'—yessir. Back home we never say 'hot' till the mercury breaks through the roof of the thermometer an' starts climbin' trees. In New York City it can be hot. Yes, sir. Sump'n fierce, but you get used to it. But hot—here! London hasn't been hot since the big fire. That's six hundred years—three, is it? Well, *then!*"

And yet he was a man who might be expected to respond to a climbing thermometer. His height was somewhere in the region of seventy-two inches, but he looked short at a distance. His girth was immense. Walking round Jim X. was exercise. He had a large pink face that had folded itself into permanent position in the course of many years. His bright blue eyes gleamed from between a pink cushion, his chins ran down in profile like the marks that men make when they try out a new fountain-pen. His hair was black and thick. Despite his fifty-five years, there was not a single grey streak. And he was something of a dandy, dressed with taste and care, invariably wore a perfectly fitting black frock coat, and a large stiff wing collar enfolded by a cravat of black satin. Amidst the folds of the cravat, which duplicated in some extraordinary fashion the puffs and creases of the face above, was invariably a pearl pin. He never wore waistcoats and was superior to suspenders. About his tremendous waist was a thin black leather belt with a golden buckle.

Mr. Orford surveyed a pleasant world from the fourth floor of Hyde Park Buildings. He could look down upon the early buddings of trees, the more vivid green of new grass, the claret and heliotrope of flowering rhododendrons and patches of scarlet and lemon flowers, the character of which he never attempted to investigate, but which were very pleasant to see. When he worked late, as he sometimes did, the faint sounds of the Park band came up to him, the "humph, humph" of the euphonium especially. Then he would draw his chair to the open window and with his hands clasped upon his belt listen emotionally and watch the shadows deepening and the lights come out and the firefly motor-cars loafing round the Park road.

The name-plate on his door as the indicator in the hall below said simply, "James X. Orford." His trade, profession, or whatever was the piece of artfulness by which he gained a living and the wherewithal to maintain himself, a staff of stenographers and various agents in and about his expensive suite, was not revealed.

His fellow-tenants in the building, men about whose means of livelihood there was no doubt, referred to him as "that American" or "that fat American." They liked him, for he was a cheerful, vital soul; they respected his mystery, and since he was an American they were a little shy of him.

There is, as Mr. Whiplow said, a certain serious earnestness about the American which is very terrifying to the English. The American makes every question an issue. He wants life and the things of life to be shaped into patterns that are agreeable one to the other. But, most curious characteristic of all, he never mocks himself. The English mock themselves all the time. It is the English form of humour that Americans never understand. They swear at themselves; they curse with remarkable bitterness the shortcomings of their rulers, but they haven't the trick of mockery which has ruined so many promising English Governments.

Mr. Orford, in the early days of his English residence, had learnt the trick.

"Set it down there, my dear," said Mr. Orford, and pointed a sausage of a finger at a small table near the open window.

His stenographer had brought him tea; not the tea that the English know, but tea poured hot upon great pebbles of ice and served in a frosted glass. This was another of the idiosyncrasies of the island he had acquired, and, acquiring, modified.

Although he employed a staff of seven, there was no member of his secretariat who had the slightest idea what was Mr. Orford's occupation. It was dimly understood that he was an "organizer," but he most certainly did not belong to that class of organizer who teaches you for a trifle how they would run your business, if they were you, and by means of brand new card-index systems and cost sheets and patent filing cabinets take the overhead charges of the factory and turn them into the overhead charges of the office.

No grateful employer of labour ever wept upon Mr. Orford's shoulder and thanked him in broken tones for having systematized his ruin.

He was not that kind of organizer.

At first they thought he had something to do with shipping. One big room of the suite contained a huge table, on the face of which was a chart of the world. On this from day to day tiny model ships were moved by a clerk trained especially for the purpose by Mr. Orford. The little world was crowded with a thousand miniature liners going east and west, south and north. Every scrap of shipping intelligence was transferred to Mr. Orford's bureau twice daily. And at least once a day James X. would come into the room and cast a keen glance over the table.

"What's the Nippon Muru boat doin' there, Stanger, hey? She's nearer Yokohama than Shanghai, I'll swear! And that Cunard boat seems to be wandering off the track—she doesn't call at the Azores. You've mixed her with a Union-Castle packet—same funnel? Yeh—but there's no U.-C. boat that's got three, you big chump. Set her up!"

All the time smiling good-naturedly.

He trained another clerk, a girl, to an understanding of the Continental railway system. He conducted a *viva voce* examination at frequent intervals.

"Man's goin' to Como, Basle, Genoa, Belgrade, Vienna. Got to meet a man for an hour at Valorbe on the outward trip and another man at Lucerne—will he have time without losing his connection? He would? You're wrong. Lucerne would kill him. Go into that, Miss Jay—you've got a crazy idea he could steal an hour by comin' back through the Gothard. It is an illusion— work it out."

In his chart-room hung huge maps of Europe showing communications, aerodromes, oil stores, coaling depôts. He could tell you to within a pound the amount of cold storage beef a man could buy at any given time in Vigo, Trieste, Dakka, Cape Town, or Colombo.

But he never bought beef, or sold ships, or dealt in railway stock. Apparently he organized nothing except the work of his office and his own amiable life.

Sitting there deep in thought, a clerk brought in a card. It was not a printed card, but the kind which Mr. Orford kept in his waiting-room for chance callers who desired to see him.

He put on his black-rimmed pince-nez and glared benevolently at the name.

"Miss Penelope Pitt," he read, and at the bottom, where the caller should have stated his or her business, "Introduction from Judge Heron, of Edmonton."

"Show that lady in," he said instantly.

Penelope came—a little nervous, very much undecided; indecision and nervous-

ness immediately overlaid by the remarkable vision which greeted her.

"Sit down there. You're from Edmonton,
eh? Got a letter? Le's see it."

He took the letter from her hand, read
it through with extraordinary rapidity, and
put it carefully by the side of his blotting-
pad. His good-humoured eyes surveyed
her searchingly, and then :

"Now, my young friend, what can I do
for you?"

With some difficulty, Penelope Pitt told
her story. In fairness to her employers, she
gave no name, did not even tell him where
she was staying.

"I feel rather like a prisoner," she said.
"In fact, I have the unpleasant sensation
that I have escaped from one of my keepers.
The lady was waiting for me at Paddington
Station, but I went down one of the sub-
ways and got out without her seeing me."

Mr. Orford's stubby fingers were clasped,
his brow was knitted.

3*

" I don't exactly know what I can do for you, Miss Pitt," he said. "And it makes it all the more awkward because I am leaving for New York on Saturday. I guess there isn't much difference between men in one part of the world or in another, and this Mr. Jones—I guess his name's not Jones, but you are trying to avoid trouble—is just the same kind of fresh thing that you'd meet in any office in New York City."

"What do you advise me to do, Mr. Orford?"

He fingered his immense chin.

"Why, I should take him at his word, Miss Pitt, and ask for your transportation back to Canada. I don't like this frankness; maybe it is part of the stock-in-trade. Does he hold any position in this country?"

She shook her head.

"His wife lives in the house, eh? Well, that makes it easier. I tell you what, Miss Pitt. There isn't much I wouldn't do for old John, or, for the matter of that, for any

Canadian girl. You wouldn't think I was Canadian, but I am. You can call this fellow's bluff, and if the money isn't forthcoming to take you back to Montreal, or to Toronto, you just call here and my clerk will fix your passage without any trouble to yourself. No, you needn't thank me, because it is unnecessary."

He raised his hand in deprecation.

"Maybe if my mind wasn't so completely occupied by a mighty serious proposition, I'd be able to give you more help, but just now only the top of my head is showing over my work, and I guess it will be snowed under before the *Olympic* pulls out of Southampton."

"It is very kind of you to want to do anything for me, Mr. Orford," she said gratefully. "I can't express my thanks, and, of course, I shall not hesitate about seeing you———"

"My head clerk," murmured Mr. Orford, and then: "If you leave the name of this smart Alec, and tell me just where you are to be found, I can do sump'n more—I see you won't. That's independence, eh? Well, maybe you're right. There's a whole lot of trouble that some people get out of without help, and I guess you are one of those people."

He offered a warm hand, and when she had gone, dismissed her from his mind, for, as he had truly said, Mr. James Xenocrates Orford was settling a mighty proposition, one which called for all his gifts as organizer, since the slightest error of judgment, a fractional mistake of timing, might mean all the difference between life and death to one in whose welfare he was inordinately interested.

" My good girl, you have given me a fright. Where on earth did you get to?" snapped Cynthia, when the girl made her appearance at Mrs. Dorban's hotel. " I thought you were lost, and I have been on the telephone to Stone House."

" I went down one of the subways," said Pen calmly, " and really I am not such a baby that I am likely to be lost in London, Cynthia. I knew your hotel."

" But what have you been doing? It is over an hour since I left Paddington!"

Penelope was not an easy liar. To satisfy the woman she told a lot of the truth, embracing, as it did, a stroll across the Park.

They were going to bed that night when Cynthia said, apropos of nothing :

" I hope Arthur's interview was satisfactory," and then, realizing she had spoken her thoughts aloud, she said : " Some friends of ours were calling on Arthur to-day."

Penelope had well realized why she had been sent for. When they returned to Stone House the next morning, Mr. Dorban was grave and preoccupied. He was even curt to her when they were alone in the study for a few minutes, and that was not Arthur Dorban's way. So remote was he in his present mood from the scene which had been enacted in the motor-boat, that she did not raise the question of her return to Canada. She realized, in fact, that she had no immediate intention of taking so drastic a step. In a way, his candour had reassured her, and put her position upon a surer foundation.

She saw very little of him, either on that day or the next. Between Arthur Dorban and his wife were a series of long and private conferences, and she was left very much to her own resources. Another unusual happening was, that Cynthia and her husband went out alone in the boat on the second afternoon, and Pen was glad to see them go.

Relieved of surveillance, she climbed up the cliff path gathering wild flowers. It was a glorious afternoon, for the heat was tempered by a breeze which blew in from the sea; the sky was an unbroken blue, the bay a painted stretch of opalescent green. It was too hot even for the gulls that from dawn to sunset screeched above Stone House.

She had reached the top of the cliff and was sitting under the shelter of a golden gorse bush, when there came to her the scent of a burning cigar. Somebody was smoking. She looked round without seeing anybody. The white beach of Borcombe was deserted. Who could it be? The people of Borcombe were not cigar smokers. Arthur Dorban confined himself to Turkish cigarettes, and, moreover, she could see the boat, and could detect his white-jerseyed figure.

She got up to her feet, and at the same

time there rose from the other side of the bush a young and chubby man. His face was red, his carefully brushed hair was the colour of sand.

"I beg your pardon," said he. "I am afraid my smoking annoyed you."

She thought he was unprepossessing, but his smile was beatific; he was unquestionably a man of education.

"I wondered where the smoke was coming from," she said with a little laugh, "but please don't stop smoking on my account."

"You are the American lady," he said quickly. "I thought it was you as I saw you coming up the path. It is strange that I didn't know you were staying at the house until to-day."

"Are you a friend of Mr. Dorban's?" she asked curiously, and his smile vanished.

"N-no," he said slowly. "I am not exactly a friend of Mr. Dorban's—I know him very well. You are staying at the house?"

"I am Mr. Dorban's secretary," she replied, and his mouth opened.

"Oh!" he said. "His secretary? Of course, that would explain everything. His servants are French," he added inconsequently.

She was a little annoyed, and he was quick to detect this.

"I am being unpardonably rude," he said, "but the fact is—I am rather interested in Dorban. I suppose Mr. Whiplow is not staying?"

"Mr. Whiplow?" she said in surprise.

"Oh, of course, you wouldn't have met him. You were in town, weren't you? Yes." He nodded wisely.

There was something so boyishly naïve about his inquisitorial methods that she half smiled.

"Yes, Whiplow went yesterday; he only stayed for the day."

"I suppose you haven't a photograph of him? I missed him by ten minutes, or I'd have snapped him. I feel rather like a fool asking you such a question, but you haven't any photograph—garden group or anything of that kind?"

She could only look at him in amazement.

"Really, I cannot discuss Mr. Dorban's visitors with you," she said, a little stiffly.

"No, of course not." He was at once apologetic. "I am being very boorish; I am so sorry!"

He turned as though to go, but waited, and she wondered what he was going to say next.

"I am staying at the Crown in Torquay," he said. He was still apologetic. "It is stupid of me to suggest that you might— but in case—my name is Stamford——"

"Mills!" she finished.

His blue eyes opened wide.

"Stamford Mills—then you have heard of me?" he asked.

She did not answer.

This was the man whom Cynthia had said was her husband's mortal enemy. He did not look very formidable, she thought.

"I am not very popular with the Dorbans," he admitted, with that slow smile of his, "and I suppose you've been warned against me." His eyes wandered out to sea, and suddenly, "Excuse me," he said, and set off at a run for the other end of the bushes.

She wondered what this extraordinary haste could portend. Presently he reappeared with a large, powerful pair of prismatic glasses, and without a word fixed them on the edge of the sea. Steadily he gazed for fully a minute, and then he put them down with a sigh.

"That wasn't bad to see her with the naked eye," he said complacently, and pointed.

Following the direction of his finger she saw far out on the horizon a tiny speck.

"You will see her better with these."

He handed the glasses to the girl, and she took and focussed them. It was some time before she could pick up the object, but presently she saw a long black ship with two high masts and a black funnel. It seemed to be stationary.

"Jolly old *Polyantha*," murmured Mr. Stamford Mills, and struck himself on the mouth as though he had committed some blazing indiscretion.

"I saw her yesterday," she said calmly as she handed the glasses to him. "She is a yacht, isn't she?"

He took some time to consider before he answered.

"Yes, she's a yacht. Belongs to a very great friend of mine, the Duc d'Augille. I have taken several voyages on her; she's quite a good ship."

He put on his hat, and then abruptly turned and walked across the common, leaving her with the impression that she had met somebody who was not quite mentally sound.

When she saw Cynthia at tea, she did not speak of the meeting, but later, the matter being on her conscience, she made a casual reference to the strange young man.

"Mills?" said Mr. Dorban with sudden violence. "What is he doing here? Did he ask you any questions?"

"Yes, he was rather inquisitive."

"I thought you said he was in London?" Arthur Dorban's tone to his wife was dictatorial and menacing.

"They told me he was in London."

"What is he doing down here? Did he speak of anybody?"

"He asked me if Mr. Whiplow had been staying."

The man and woman exchanged glances.

"You told him, of course, that we had never had anybody here called Whiplow?"

"He seemed to think you had a visitor yesterday," said Pen. "Even I had that illusion."

Dorban plied her with questions, and the keener he became, the less inclined she seemed to give him details of the conversation.

Of the *Polyantha* she did not speak at all; it was so trivial and incidental that it hardly seemed worth while repeating.

It was late on the following afternoon that Cynthia gave the girl a little task which she had mentioned once or twice before.

"I wish you would empty the trunk in the lumber-room," she said. "Any time will do. It has a lot of summer frocks of mine that I think could be sold. I had a card from a wardrobe dealer in Torquay who wants to buy old dresses, and I might as well sell them as leave them to the moths."

"You have spoken about that before. I'll go right away and do it," said Pen. She

came back to Cynthia after a few minutes
absence, with a request for keys.

"Is it locked?" said Cynthia in surprise.
"I don't remember locking it." She pulled
open a drawer of her little secretaire and
took out a bunch of keys. "One of these
will fit, I think," she said, and Penelope
went back to her task. She had no difficulty
in finding a key, and opened the lid.

The trunk was a large green one, and
Cynthia had once, in showing her over the
house the day after her arrival, told her
that it was one of two she had bought, its
fellow having been lost in transit on the
railway.

The tray on the top was empty, and she
pulled it out and laid it on the floor. A
sheet of brown paper covered the contents,
and this also she removed. On the top of
the trunk's contents lay two unframed etchings. One was the head of a saint, and the
other a landscape in the Corot manner.

Attached by a clip was a paper, which fell to the floor as she took out the engravings, expecting to find dresses underneath. She picked it up; it was a receipt—" Received the sum of £700, in payment for my two original etchings, the ' Head of Mark' and ' A View in Brittany.' " It was signed " John Feltham," and the date was exactly a year before.

She laid down the engravings, put the receipt on the attic window-sill, which was within reach of her hand, removed another sheet of paper, and sank back on her heels paralyzed with astonishment, for beneath the paper was package after package of Bank of England notes. They were notes of all denominations, from five to a hundred pounds. So staring, she heard an exclamation behind her, and turned to meet the white face of Cynthia.

" My God !" said the woman in a whisper.

Before Penelope could speak, Cynthia had

caught her by the arm and dragged her to her feet and into the passage.

"Go down and tell——" But there was no need to summon Arthur Dorban; he had followed his wife up the stairs.

"You fool!" hissed Cynthia. "You damnable fool! *You sank the wrong trunk!*"

AFTER a gloomy dinner Penelope walked in the garden trying to collect her thoughts, striving to unravel the tangled mystery of the Dorbans' lives. He had sunk the wrong trunk! Was that the trunk that Cynthia had said had been lost in transit on the railway? And why should they sink a trunk full of banknotes to a fabulous value?

They had not attempted to explain a single thing to her, and that was ominous. The air was charged with electricity. There was danger; she knew it, she felt it.

Cynthia's sharp voice called her in the gathering gloom, and she went slowly, and with a heart that beat a little faster, to meet the unknown. As she passed along the path which bordered the house she saw a flutter of something white at her feet, and stooping, picked up a paper. Even in the half-light she knew that it was the receipt she had seen; it must have been blown by the wind from the ledge above. She put the paper in the pocket of the knitted jersey she wore, intending to restore it.

"Come in here, Penelope," said Cynthia's metallic voice, and she followed the woman into the small drawing-room.

Arthur Dorban was sitting at a small table, his long chin resting in the palm of his hand. He did not look up as they entered, but kept his eyes fixed upon the lace table-centre.

Penelope heard the click of the door as it closed behind her, and knew that she was a prisoner.

"Here she is," said Cynthia harshly.

Still her husband made no sign of movement.

"Well, tell her." Cynthia's impatience was not disguised.

Then it was that Arthur Dorban looked up.

"I'll tell her alone," he said.

Mrs. Dorban shrugged her thin shoulders.

"I could bear it," she said ironically, and then took a step toward her husband, leaning down over him. "You know what there is in this, Slico," she said. "There are going to be no halfways or compromises, you understand? If you haven't the heart for it, I have!"

He nodded, and, looking at him again for a moment, the woman turned and stepped from the room.

Not until the door closed did he look up, and Penelope saw him wetting his lips with the tip of his tongue.

"I gave you a chance the other day of getting back to Canada, and I wish to God you'd taken it. You can't go back to Canada now or anywhere else. There is only one chance, but it is not the chance that Cynthia thinks. You remember what I said to you in the boat?"

She nodded. Her mouth was bone dry;

she could not have articulated had she tried.

"That's the way out for you," he said, "but it means we've got to settle with Cynthia."

"I don't quite understand what you mean. What have I done?" she asked huskily.

"You have seen something you shouldn't have seen, and if you knew more about what had happened in this country during the last twelve months, you wouldn't ask that question. I'm tired of Cynthia; I told you that before. And I've got to choose between Cynthia and you. And one of you has— got to go out!"

Her eyes, wide with horror, searched his face.

"Go out?" she said slowly.

"That's the size of it," he nodded. Suddenly he was on his feet beside her, and she stood paralyzed with terror. His arm was about her shoulder, his hand underneath her chin. "Look at me," he whispered, and now his eyes were blazing. "I'd go to the scaffold for you, if you say the word, but you've got to be in it, do you hear? I was cold enough on the boat, wasn't I? You don't know what it meant to me to hold myself in, Penelope. I want you. I want you more than I want anything in the world." His hot lips pressed hers, and suddenly the spell was broken, and she thrust him back. Turning, she ran swiftly from the room into the darkened hall; her hand was on the balustrade of the stairs when something passed over her face. She knew it was a silk scarf long before it had tightened on her throat. She tried to scream, but the sound was strangled, and she was flung to the floor.

She had never fainted before; she did not know she had fainted until she recovered consciousness to find herself back in the drawing-room, with her hands tied tightly together.

"If you scream you will be sorry for yourself," said Cynthia. The woman's face was drawn and haggard; her eyes seemed to have sunk into her head, and Pen would not have recognized her.

Turning her head, she saw Arthur Dorban standing with folded arms, his face black with gloom.

"Get up," said Cynthia curtly, and the girl struggled to her feet.

Cynthia looked at the watch on her wrist, and, taking up the scarf from the table, wound it round and round the girl's mouth.

Pen knew that it was useless to resist or struggle; she could only wait and husband her strength for the final test. She tried to pull her hands, to loosen them so that one could be slipped through, but her efforts were in vain. Mrs. Dorban must have guessed her thoughts, for she smiled crookedly.

"You won't get out of that, my girl," she said. "Let me see." She peered down. "No, the silk will show no marks," she said, relieved. "Come, come!" She took the girl's arm in hers and led her to the door.

"Wait!" cried Dorban hoarsely.

Cynthia turned and her eyes narrowed.

"I will come back and talk to you, Slico," she said softly.

Outside in the garden Cynthia spoke again.

"If you make a fuss you will get hurt, my dear," she said. "Look at this!"

The moon was obscured by a heavy bank of clouds, but there was enough light to see the little automatic in Cynthia Dorban's hand.

Pen nodded, and together they walked down the garden path, through the doorway in the wall, and with the older woman gripping her arm, they passed down the steps and came to a halt on the flat rock of the boathouse.

Cynthia pulled open the narrow door which led to the interior.

"Get into the boat," she said, and Penelope obeyed.

It seemed like a bad dream; she kept telling herself that it could not be true. Presently she would wake up. And yet all the time she knew that she was experiencing a ghastly reality. She stumbled into the boat, and Cynthia followed her, stooping to loosen the moorings before she started the engine. Slowly the motor-boat glided out along the rocky reef to the open bay, Cynthia at the wheel, the girl crouched at her feet, frozen with horror.

The moon emerged from its cloudy screen and threw a strange green light over the sea. Along the shore the night lights were twinkling; a profound silence reigned on the world, a silence broken only by the rhythmical beating of the propeller.

The boat ran for twenty minutes at full speed, and then Cynthia stopped the engine. She went forward, returning with a coil of rope, one end of which she passed round the girl's waist and scientifically knotted. Then she bent down, and Penelope heard

4

the jangle of the iron bars which were kept in the bottom of the boat for ballast. She took out two thick square ingots and laid them at Penelope's feet. These she knotted together with a spare rope, the loose ends of which she tied tightly about the girl's feet.

And then the full realization of the horror that this woman contemplated came upon the girl, and she nearly fainted again. She bit her lips until the blood came. It was a dream, it could not be true; no human man or woman could be guilty of so fiendish a crime. Yet she reasoned, automatically, that year by year crimes as ferocious had been laid at the door of women. But it wasn't true, it couldn't be true—she was mad to think—presently she would wake up.

"I am going to drop you over the side," Cynthia was saying calmly, "and when you are dead I will bring you up and take the weights from your feet——"

Pen screamed, but the silk scarf muffled her voice, and the woman jerked her to her feet. For a second they stood, victim and executioner, and then Penelope, gathering all her strength for the effort, flung herself violently against the murderess. Cynthia staggered for a moment, clawed wildly to recover her balance—— There was a scream and a splash, and the girl looked round to see the woman's head reappear above the water and the white flash of her hands as she struck out for the boat. She tried to move forward, but the irons held her. Bending down, she gripped the rope in her swollen hands and pulled with all her might. She was within reach of the starting-lever; the engines were running silently; she flung all her weight and swung the lever forward. Instantly, with a splutter and a turmoil of waters, the boat moved on.

Again she looked back. Cynthia was swimming. She remembered that Dorban had told her that she swam like a fish. Pulling down the scarf that covered her mouth, the girl breathed in the night air with long, painful gulps. She was trembling in every limb, her head was swimming. First, she must remove the horrible irons from her ankles, and, sitting down, she plucked at the knots with trembling fingers. Presently she was free, but her hands were still bound. Leaving the engines running, she made her way forward. In one of the lockers under the seat was a little store of cutlery and table-linen, which the Dorbans used for picnics. She wrenched open the door of the locker and presently found a knife. Sitting down on the floor, with the knife between her feet, she sawed at the bonds until her hands were free.

Her first thought, on returning to the wheel, was to throw the hateful irons over-board, and she experienced a foolish relief when they had disappeared over the side. Cynthia was no longer in sight. She peered back toward the shore, but she could see nothing.

Where was she going? She was heading

for the open sea without thought of danger. The real danger lay behind her. She wanted to get away, away, away! Perhaps she could round Portland Bill; Weymouth lay beyond, and Weymouth was a long distance from Borcombe. The thought comforted her.

Still she could not believe it was all real, though the pain in her wrists told her she was awake.

And then her practical mind asserted itself, and she searched the boat, making an inventory of the boat's stores. There was sufficient gasolene for a day's cruise, but there was no food or water on board. Still, she was so close to the land that that did not worry her very much.

She guessed the hour to be eleven. She would be in Weymouth by daybreak. She did not feel a bit sleepy until nearly midnight, and then reaction and physical exhaustion overcame her; she could hardly keep her eyes open. But she was soon wide awake again, for without warning she ran into a bank of fog.

Again she searched the boat, this time for a compass, but in vain. The sane thing to do, she thought, was to stop the engines and drop anchor until the fog cleared, for just before the fog had come she was nearly abreast of the Portland Light, and it seemed a simple matter to feel along the coast listening for breakers. She checked the engines to half-speed and moved on and on. Then, as suddenly, she ran out of the fog. There was no land in sight; in the eastern skies the grey of dawn was showing, and right ahead of her was a ship which was moving slowly, and had evidently just emerged from one of those patchy fog banks which embarrass the summer navigation of the Channel. But at the sight of the ship her heart bounded. Here was safety, and she rose and shouted.

She heard a voice on the bridge, and suddenly she was blinded by a light which

flashed upon her, a dazzling white search-
light which held her and her tiny craft in
cold scrutiny. She shouted again, and a
voice from the bridge said :

"*Come under the stern to the port gangway!*"

It was the hollow, booming voice of a
man speaking through a megaphone. She
set the engines going and brought the little
motor-boat under the stern of the ship, and,
looking up, she saw the dull gold of letters
which she could not distinguish. A minute
later the boat was swaying by the side of a
hastily lowered gangway, and a seaman
pulled her to the little platform at the foot
of the steps.

"Bring the woman aboard, but cast off the
boat."

Half-fainting as she was, the girl could
only stare her astonishment as, with a thrust
of the seaman's foot, the motor-boat was cast
adrift. Her knees were shaking as she was
led up on to the deck. In the light of a

lamp a man was standing; he was dressed in violet pyjamas, and he was of a tremendous size.

"Sump'n wrong, eh?" he bellowed. "Sump'n the matter?"

The girl recognized him instantly.

"Oh, Mr. Orford!" she wailed, and fell sobbing hysterically upon his broad chest.

"Sump'n wrong here," mumbled Mr. James Xenocrates Orford. "What in thunder are you doing on my *Polyantha?*"

WHEN Pen awoke in the morning she was
in a large and airy cabin. It was also a
very luxurious cabin, she noted idly, as her
eyes wandered around. The hangings were
of a delicate blue silk; the bed on which she
lay (it was not a bunk) appeared to be of
silver. On the floor was a thick blue carpet,
and the room was panelled in rosewood.
There was a pretty little inlaid writing-table,
and a silver reading-lamp; a deep and roomy
armchair was placed within reach of three
shelves filled with books in leather bindings.

She did not remember coming to bed;
she was not undressed. Somebody had
loosened her skirt about the waist, and had
taken off her shoes. She did not want to
get up; she just wanted to lie and listen
to the monotonous thud of the screw and to
enjoy that gentle swaying motion which was

so soothing. She was on a ship, and she really did not wish to think about how she got there. And yet in a calm, deliberate, and cold-blooded fashion she recalled without a tremor or shudder all that had happened on the night before. She wondered what time it was, and just as she wondered a bell struck almost over her head.

One bell—that must be half-past eight.

Still she did not attempt to move, not even to pull aside the silken quilt which had been laid over her. At that moment there was a tap at the door.

"Come in," she said, and was surprised to hear how weak her voice sounded. She expected to see a stewardess, but it was a blue-jerseyed sailor who came in answer to her summons. He was a tall sailor, his face tanned to a deep mahogany. The first thing she noticed was that he was remarkably good-looking, even if his manners were not perfect, for he did not attempt to remove his flat-crowned hat.

" I. have brought you a cup of tea," he said. "I am not sure that you take sugar, and I suppose the correct thing would have been to bring the tray with all its necessary paraphernalia—that did not occur to me until I was halfway here." He put the cup down gingerly upon the table by the side of the bed, and she was too astonished to make any observation.

She had never associated sailors with gentle speech and a certain precision of language. His hands were rough and hard, his clothes were a thought shabby; but he carried himself and spoke like a gentleman.

" Thank you very much," she said, and struggled to her elbow. " Will you tell the stewardess I would like to see her?"

" I am the stewardess," he said gravely, and in spite of her throbbing head she laughed.

" Who brought me here last night?" she asked.

" I brought you here," said the solemn

young man. "You were so fast asleep that
it was impossible to wake you. I took the
liberty of loosening your—er—clothing."
He looked at her with even greater gravity.
" I was very happy to discover that you do
not wear corsets," he said. " That would
have been a great embarrassment. If you
permit me, I will prepare your bath."

In one corner of the cabin was a door
which she had not noticed, and through this
he disappeared. She heard the splash of
running water, and after a while he came
back.

" I have cleaned your shoes," he said.
" We have everything on the ship that you
are likely to require, except a change of
clothing. We hope to manage this for you
later."

" Where am I?" she asked.

" You are on the good ship *Polyantha*."

" *Polyantha!*" Wasn't that the boat that
Mr. Stamford Mills had seen? She remembered now. It was an extraordinary co-

incidence. "I must dress before we get into harbour or port, or wherever we are going," she said. "If you will get me a needle and thread, I will try to make myself presentable."

He coughed behind his hand.

"We are not going into harbour. I feel you ought to know this. We are on a long voyage."

She stared at him.

"But surely you could put me ashore?"

He shook his head.

"I fear that we cannot even put you ashore," he said in his sober way.

"But I can't go on a long voyage. I'm not prepared—and besides——"

"You can wireless to your friends that you are safe," he said.

It occurred to Penelope Pitt at that moment that she had no friends with whom she could communicate.

"Was I dreaming, or was it Mr. Orford I saw last night?"

"It was Mr. Orford," said the other precisely.

"Is he going to America on this ship?" she asked, relieved.

"He is not going to America. He is at this precise moment going to breakfast."

With a little bow he turned and walked out of the cabin, closing the door after him. He opened it again for a second.

"You may bolt the door, and, curiously enough, the lock of the cabin is in working order. As a rule the locks of cabin doors are never in working order. You will find the key in the top right-hand drawer of the writing-desk."

An extraordinary young man, thought Penelope, revelling in the luxury of a hot bath. When she opened the door of the cabin later she found her shoes on the deck outside. The cabin opened upon the upper deck. A stiff breeze was blowing, and to prevent her flimsy footwear from being blown overboard, the " stewardess " had laid

an iron pin across them. At the sight of
the iron she shivered.

Ten minutes later she stepped out on to
the deck.

"Good-morning, Miss Pitt."

She turned with a start.

A plump young man was enjoying her
astonishment.

"Aren't you Mr. Stamford Mills?" she
asked.

"That is my name," said he. "I had the
pleasure of meeting you yesterday."

"But—but——" she stammered. "Why
are you here?"

"Won't you meet our doctor, Dr.
Fraser?"

Dr. Fraser was a taciturn Scotsman with a
disapproving eye. She could not help feeling that Dr. Fraser regarded her presence on that ship as something in the nature
of an outrage, and it occurred to her to ask
if there were any other ladies on the yacht.

"There are no others," said Mr. Robert

Stamford Mills, "and how you came here
is a mystery to me. I heard nothing about
it until I woke up this morning, and then
they told me they had picked you up at sea
in a small motor-boat. What on earth were
you doing out in the middle of the night?"

"I was being murdered," said Pen calmly.

Bobby Mills' face changed.

"Murdered?" he said quickly. "What do
you mean?"

She shook her head.

"If I told you, you would think I was
insane, because such things do not happen
except in mad dreams or in mad books. I
am not going to tell anybody till I get
ashore, and then I am not so certain——"

"But you must tell me," he said authorita-
tively, and then, seeing her stiffen, "or Mr.
Orford."

"Do you know Mr. Orford?" she asked
in surprise, and then: "Of course you do.
Why is Mr. Orford here? I thought he
was going to America."

"Was it Cynthia or Arthur?" persisted Bobby Mills. "And why? Did you find out something about them, or——"

"What?" she challenged.

He bit his lip thoughtfully.

"Cynthia Dorban is an intensely jealous woman, and a woman without the slightest compassion. Her first husband died in curious circumstances, and my own opinion is——" He stopped himself.

"Here is Mr. Orford," she interrupted him, and Bobby went to meet that stout, jovial man. Presently the two came back to where she was standing by the rail.

"Well, I must say that I didn't reckon on you," Orford greeted her, without visible signs of annoyance. "Do you know what you are, young lady? You are a little bit of grit in the smooth machinery of my organization. You are the fifth wheel and the ninth dimension. You don't belong here. You are just like a loose paper wandering around pigeon-holes that don't fit you.

Sump 'n has got to be done about you. Yes,
sir."

"Am I so much in the way?" she asked
guiltily.

Mr. Orford took off his hat and rubbed his
thick hair irritably.

"You may be," he said cautiously. "For
the minute, you are no more in the way than
a blooming rose in the desert of Arabia.
You are the pink hat at the funeral, and
naturally you are considerably conspicuous,
and that's what is worrying me."

"Can't you put me ashore?" she asked.

He shook his big head.

"No, ma'am, I can't put you ashore," he
said decidedly. "There ain't any shore to
put you to. You are just going to wander
round the Wes'n ocean like a lil' sea urchin,
that's what! And maybe it is right and
providential that you happened. You kind
of supply the credentials of the party, but
we've got no clothes for you, no face powder
or eyebrow pencil or hair wash. You are in

a severely masculine environment, and until we strike the Southern Pacific, I can't see what we can do for you, unless——" He looked at the other, pursed his lips and closed his eyes. "You've a pretty thin chance of getting so much as a falderal from *her*."

Pen wondered who the mysterious "her" was. She could not guess that the "her" was an oilship which he chartered and which was to meet them at sea.

"Now, young lady," he said. He put his arm about her shoulder paternally, and took her aft to where the big red-cushioned deck-chairs were. "You are going to tell me just what happened and just why you are here."

"I am afraid I can't, Mr. Orford," she said, shaking her head. "The matter is now so serious that I can't tell anybody, unless I am prepared to tell the police also."

"Bad as that, eh?" He mused, looking at her searchingly through the slits of his eyes. " Mrs. Dorban, too, Bobby tells me. Was it Mr. Dorban who you complained was getting fresh with you? I see," he nodded. " It wouldn't be for that. Did she try to kill you? You needn't tell me, I can see she did. I never thought she was that kind. People don't go so far, only one in eighty-three thousand seven hundred and forty-five have a murderer's mind, and I guess you struck one of the ones! Now tell me straight, man to man, Miss Pitt—what's your other name, by the way? Penelope, kind of companion to Xenocrates, eh?—tell me what was the cause of it all."

" I've told you too much already," said Pen with an obstinate tilt of her chin. " I do not want to figure in a police trial, and in any circumstances it would be a very difficult charge to prove."

He nodded.

" If I know that lady," he said, "she is already filing an affidavit that you tried to murder *her*—she's that kind. Lordy! If I had only known that you were in the Dorbans' house !"

"What difference would it have made?" she asked, but he was no more in a mind to give her his confidence than she was to speak frankly to him.

She went back to her cabin soon after and found her nice sailor making the bed. To her practised eye, he looked like a man who had made many beds before, and she stood watching him, he unknowing, as with deft hands he arranged sheet and blanket and coverlet, put a new slip upon the pillow and turned back the sheet neatly.

" Thank you," she said, and he started and turned. Only for a second was he embarrassed.

" I think your cabin is shipshape now, miss," he said.

" By the way, what is your name?" asked the girl.

He scratched his chin.

"What is my name?" he repeated. " To

tell you the truth, Miss Pitt, I haven't given the matter a thought. How would John suit me?"

"John it shall be," she said good-humouredly.

He paused at the door.

"Is there anything you want? We have no flowers on board, but if you would like a little greenery, we have some carrots in cold storage, and I dare say we could fix up——"

"I don't even want greenery," she said, just a little piqued by his familiarity. She was ashamed of herself immediately after he had gone.

To her surprise, luncheon was served in her cabin. Apparently her fellow-passengers had no particular desire to meet her at meals. John, who served the lunch, had, however, another explanation.

"They think you might feel awkward if you were the only lady present at eats," he said. "You'll be seeing the captain after lunch. He isn't a bad fellow, but somewhat devoid of humour—and yet he's a Scot!"

He took her breath away with his easy manner. She had always been under the impression that the ship's captain was a being of whom every sailor man stood in awe, and she was doubly surprised when at last she met Captain Willit, for that gentleman was a fierce-looking old man who glowered at her from under overhanging white eyebrows, and made an excuse at the earliest opportunity for leaving her.

She discovered that the *Polyantha* was an oil-burning yacht, and that the crew was a small one. There were many curious things about the vessel which she did not understand. Not the least curious was the attitude of the guests and officers towards her steward, John. Nobody ever spoke to him, and if he, as he frequently did, ventured a casual or jocular comment upon a situation which had arisen, they looked past and ignored him. None the less, he seemed to thrive on

the somewhat chilly atmosphere in which he
lived.

The second remarkable member of the
crew was a sailor who apparently did nothing
but sit in the well of the foredeck, smoking
an interminable chain of cigars. He was a
broad-shouldered, bullet-headed man, with a
brutal face. He looked like a prize-fighter
with his close-cropped head, his snub nose,
and heavy jowl. His idle indolence would
have alone attracted her attention, but even
more remarkable was the fact that round his
waist was a belt in which hung two long-
barrelled revolvers, one at either hip.

He looked up as she was leaning over the
rail, watching him, and the queer contortion
of face which was intended to be a smile
made him even more unpleasant to look
upon. And then, to her indignation, he deliberately winked at her. At first she thought
it was accidental, but when he put up his
hand and blew her a kiss, she turned away.

"What is the matter?"

It was her steward.

"That sailor," she said, a little incoherently. "He—he—— Oh, it was nothing. I suppose sailors are like that." She tried to smile through her annoyance, but he was not deceived.

"Has he been offensive?" asked John.

"He was a little—blew me a kiss. I suppose he thought I was——"

But before she could finish, he had turned and run down the companion-way to the lower deck. She saw him walk quickly toward the big man, and then a stranger thing happened. The man with the brutal face sprang to his feet, dropped both hands upon the protruding butts of his pistols, and whipped them out. She saw the two men speaking, and presently John turned and his face was white. He came up the ladder more slowly than he had gone down.

"He won't bother you again," he said shortly, and walked past her.

THE idle sailor's name was Hollin; she learnt this from Bobby Mills, but that young gentleman seemed quite unwilling to discuss the man or his idiosyncrasies.

"Why does he wear those revolvers?"

"I can't imagine," said Bobby politely. "Probably he is one of those sad cases of men who have been influenced by the horrible movies."

Toward evening Hollin appeared on the upper deck. A cigar was stuck in the corner of his mouth, his hands were in his pockets, and he lounged along the deck to the far end, to disappear down the companion-way.

Not one of the guests took the slightest notice of him. The old captain, who was standing by Orford's chair, merely glared at him as he passed, but offered no reproof. Yet with the other members of the crew the strictest discipline was maintained. The quartermasters saluted in navy fashion and moved at the double whenever the watch officer's whistle sounded. Only John and the swaggering Hollin seemed superior to the laws of the sea, but in fairness to John, he appeared to do nothing to which offence might be taken, apart from his passion for butting into conversations.

Mr. Orford spent the greater part of the day asleep in one of the deep chairs in the after-deck, a big sun umbrella rigged over him.

The second of the guests, Mr. Mills, appeared to find occupation in his own cabin.

Orford and Mills were apparently the only passengers on the yacht. There were the first, second, and third officers, the chief engineer and his one assistant, a purser, about twelve hands, and the captain.

The only disturbance to the serenity of the ship came when the wireless operator appeared with something written on a slip

of paper. Then there would be a hasty
conference, grouped about Mr. James Xenocrates Orford, who was aroused for the
occasion and became instantly wide awake.

Once, after such a conference, the course
of the *Polyantha* was altered, the ship, which
had been heading for the setting sun, swung
round and pursued a course due south. And
they were going faster, the girl noticed. The
decks shivered again, and the *Polyantha*
began to take little seas over her sharp-
pointed bow. Then, without warning, the
course was changed east, then south again.

Early in the afternoon a man had climbed
up to the crow's nest on the foremast, and
had spent his watch scanning the horizon
with a telescope. That night everybody was
glum and silent. Bobby answered any observation she made to him in monosyllables.
Mr. Orford sat in silence, his hands crossed
over his stomach. She thought he was
asleep, but James Xenocrates Orford was
very much awake.

The only cheerful person on board was John, the steward. He served her dinner, and brought her coffee to the deck. When she retired that night she found him squatting on the deck with his back to the superstructure, and he rose silently as she appeared.

"Is there anything I can get you before you go to bed, Miss Pitt?"

"No, thank you, John," she said.

"I have put some mineral water in your cabin. I think I told you that there is a key to the door. What time would you like your tea to-morrow? I am afraid that you will have to come to the door and get it. I am an excellent steward, but a bashful chambermaid. How are they aft?"

He jerked his head in the direction of her fellow-passengers.

"They are not very bright," she confessed. "Can you tell me, John, where we are going?"

"I haven't the faintest idea," he replied.

" Through the Panama Canal perhaps, to the South Sea Islands."

"Whose ship is this?"

"I forget the name of the gentleman; he's a French Duke, but the gentleman who has chartered the yacht is the chaste Xenocrates."

" Mr. Orford?" she said in surprise.

" Mr. Orford," said John, nodding.

" Do you know him very well?"

" Never met him in my life till I saw him on board this ship," said John promptly. "You were going to say something at that minute? I wonder if I know what it was. Weren't you going to ask me why a man of my superior attainments and conversational powers should be engaged in a menial capacity upon Mr. Orford's yacht?"

" I did think it strange," she confessed.

"Very strange," he said emphatically, "very strange. You would be a blasé-minded old lady if you thought it was any-thing *but* strange. I don't exactly know how

I am going to explain my presence to you, except by producing a hypothesis which may or may not hypothecate. Imagine a poor Scottish student who utilizes his vacation by going to sea in order to pay his college fees. Does that convince you?"

"No, it doesn't," she said, and then, realizing that perhaps the conversation had gone far enough, she bade him good-night and went in.

He heard the key turn in the lock, and strode down to the well-deck. A dark figure squatting on a bollard rose with alacrity.

"Put those stupid guns away, my good friend," said John testily, "and go to bed. Why aren't you in bed?"

"Because I ain't going to bed until you are in bed," said the other. His voice was hoarse and cracked. "That's why, Mr. Clever! I ain't going to let nobody put one over on me. I know the right of my position. I've been thinking it over, matey, and I'll tell you what it's going to be. It is going to cost that fat bloke twenty thousand. Not a penny less. Twenty thousand, and me landed in South America."

John took a cigarette from his trouser pocket and lit it.

"You're a beast," he said briefly, and was turning away when the man spoke again.

"Here, matey," he asked, lowering his voice, "who's that skirt?"

"That what?" John swung round.

"That skirt in the cabin up above? I see her come aboard last night. Who is she, matey? She's as pretty as a picture." He smacked his thick lips.

"Hollin!" John's voice was soft. "Do you really want to get to South America? If so, do not mention that lady again. And listen! If you do any more kiss-throwing I'll get you in spite of your guns. You'll not be looking the way the bullet will come, remember that, Hollin."

"What's the good of talking like that, matey?" whined the man. "Ain't I behaved

like a gentleman all through the piece?
Didn't I scrag Crawley when he'd have got
you?"

"You're a liar," said the other without
heat. "There was no need to scrag
Crawley——"

Pen's cabin was flush with the rail of the
foredeck; two portholes overlooked the well
where the two men were talking, and those
portholes were open. She had been standing, her elbow resting upon the casings,
looking out into the blue-green moonlit sea,
and there had come to her the murmur of
sound, and then she had heard John speaking distinctly.

"Scrag Crawley." Who was the unfortunate Crawley—for scragging was obviously
something distinctly unpleasant? And what
had these two men, so strangely diverse, in
common with one another?

Presently the voices died away, and after
a visit to the door to make sure that it was
locked, she crept into her bed, and in a

5

few minutes was fast asleep. Once in the night she woke with a start. The ship was listing over so much that only the silver guards of her bed kept her from rolling to the floor. She got up in some alarm, but immediately afterwards the *Polyantha* righted herself. Pulling back the curtains which covered the windows, she looked out. Far away on the horizon she saw a twinkle of light, and as she looked there came to her ears a rattle and clang which for the moment startled her, till she recalled the fact that the navigating bridge was above her head, and that the sound she had heard was the ship's telegraph.

She pushed the port open wider, and then she heard the captain's voice.

"There she is. We have been getting her signals for two hours. Do you think she saw us?"

"No, the light didn't come within ten miles of us. What time is it?" asked a deep voice, which she recognized as Mr. Orford's.

"Nearly two. We have an hour and a half before daybreak. We are doing twenty-six knots now, and unless she takes it into her head to follow our course, we'll be out of sight."

There was a long silence, and she thought the men must have gone to the chart-house.

Suddenly Mr. Orford's voice asked :
"What was that?"

"An aeroplane," said the other laconically. "I heard it an hour ago. Are all lights out, Simpson?"

"Switched off from the main, sir," said a third voice.

"Navigating lights out?"

"Yes, sir."

"Go along both decks and see if any of the watch are smoking." Then in a different voice : "Engine-room—that you, Ferly? Is there any possibility of light showing from the funnels? If there is, take whatever action is necessary."

The thud of the screws suddenly ceased and there was silence.

Now Pen heard the sound. It was a drone that developed into a noise such as a circular saw makes when it is cutting through hard wood. It passed and died down again. Another long interval of silence, and a soft patter of feet above her head, and then she heard a fourth voice.

"Just come through, sir, from an Admiralty broadcast."

"What is it?" growled the captain.

The man was evidently reading by memory, for there could be no light upon the bridge.

"To all ocean-going traffic, Dungeness to Land's End. Please report instantly by radio to Admiralty if wreck of an aeroplane has been sighted by your ship."

"Damn Hollin and his cap. I knew that swine would spoil everything!"

Penelope came back to her bed and sat on its edge, her arms folded, her pretty face puckered in a frown. Now she knew the reason the ship had listed. They had again changed the direction, and she recalled the fact that when in the day this had happened, the *Polyantha* laid over lazily upon the side to which they had turned. Of what were they afraid? Why were all the lights out? The *Polyantha* held a secret—a secret associated with Hollin and his cap. She laughed helplessly and went to bed. Just as she was falling asleep the telegraph rattled and rang again, and she heard the engines going at full speed.

She remembered nothing more until a discreet knock came upon her door, and the voice of John demanded :

"Do you mind preserved milk? Our cow is not quite herself this morning."

THE second day of *Polyantha* broke grey
and chilly. The sea had lost its unruffled
smoothness, and throughout the day they
ran into rain squalls at regular intervals.

Pen was glad of her jersey, and when
John produced a man's overcoat of blanket
cloth, she accepted his kindness gratefully,
and allowed him to turn up the sleeves for
her, and button it under her chin.

"It is the smallest coat on board," explained John. "I think it belongs to Bobby
Mills."

"You don't call him 'Bobby' to his face,
do you?" asked the interested girl.

"I never call him anything to his face,"
said John coolly. "It happens to be his
name, and I can't go round 'mistering'
people all the time. It is so very

monotonous, apart from being extremely snobbish. I think Bobby is a name which suits him rather well. He is the greatest fellow on earth, as straight as a die——"

"You seem to know him rather well."

"I know of him. Everybody knows Stamford Mills by repute, even an obscure Aberdeen student. By the way, did we agree that that should be my rôle?"

"We did not," she said severely.

"Very good. What will you have for breakfast? We have eggs and bacon, and bacon and eggs. We also have ham that looks like bacon. We can supply you with cutlets *à la Française* or *à la Americaine*. We have clam chowder in cans—this, I understand, being the favourite dish of the good folks of Edmonton——"

"Who told you I came from Edmonton?" she asked suspiciously.

"You did," he replied without shame. "When I was putting you to bed the other night, you were talking in your sleep——"

"John," said Penelope awfully, "you are being indelicate."

All this conversation took place through the crack of a door open no more than an inch.

Penelope told herself afterwards that it was not right to carry on what was tantamount to a flirtation with a deck hand. Of course, it was not a flirtation, or anything like a flirtation, but it might be interpreted that way. At the same time, it was rather difficult to treat John as though he were an ordinary able seaman. There was no reason, however, why she should go beyond the ordinary boundaries of courtesy, and she resolved there and then to adopt a new and less intimate attitude toward this pleasant steward of hers.

She could not be cold, and, naturally, she could not snub him. It occurred to her that, if neither of these courses were pursued, there was very little change that she could bring about. It was also annoying, in view

of her desire to stand upon another footing
with John, that he was the only person of
whom she could ask information. She had
sensed something in the placid Mr. Orford
which was not exactly hostility, but was not
enthusiastic friendship. For some reason
her arrival upon the *Polyantha* had upset a
very carefully laid plan. What that plan
could be, she considered deeply without
finding any solution. The yachting cruise
was not in the nature of a pleasure trip.
There was something sinister about it all.
She could not suspect either the chubby
Bobby Mills or the benevolent Mr. Orford
of criminal practice, and yet—what was the
meaning of that stealthy flight down the
Channel? The constant change of course,
the putting out of the lights; and Hollin,
that evil man with his cigar—what had he to
do with it, and what had his cap?

She put her hand to her throbbing temples.
The more she thought the more confused
she became. The difficulty of her own posi-

5*

tion left her unmoved. She was wholly independent, her time was her own, and it mattered very little to her whether the *Polyantha* was bound for the South Sea Islands or the Arctic regions. For here was the strange thing, that, in spite of the peculiar errand of the *Polyantha*, she felt singularly safe.

She searched in her mind trying to recall the particulars of all the sea stories she had ever read. Perhaps the *Polyantha* was in search of hidden treasure—or was it gun-running? What country was at war that would be likely to requisition the services of the *Polyantha* for that purpose? She could not remember any.

John served her lunch, and for once was almost taciturn.

Pen was irritated; she was in the mood for asking questions, and he gave her no opening, until he was clearing away the plates.

"We are running into fine weather," he

said, apropos of nothing. She glanced through the open porthole; the sky and sea were grey, and a trailing veil of rain was moving slowly across the western horizon.

"I suppose we call somewhere before we reach the South Sea Islands?" she asked.

He stopped, tray in hand.

"Did I say South Sea Islands? If I did, I was joking. I don't know where we are going. Yes, we must stop somewhere, I suppose. I don't know what the arrangements are; I haven't even bothered to ask."

"Aren't you afraid that you will be rather late for the opening of your college term?" she asked sarcastically, and he smiled.

"I dare say they'll postpone the opening if I am not back," said he.

"John." She called him when he was at the door, and he put down the tray on the deck outside and came back empty-handed. "Do you know what is the mystery of the *Polyantha*?"

"The only mystery on the *Polyantha* is

you," he said. "All women are more or less mysterious——"

"Don't be silly," she said impatiently. "Why are we sneaking—there is no other word for it—away from England? There is something very strange about this voyage."

"Does it worry you?" he asked quickly, and she considered.

"Not very much. It piques me. I hate being kept in the dark, and I am a little worried about Mrs.—a lady."

"The lady who tried to throw you overboard from her motor-boat?" he finished. "Well, you needn't trouble about that sweet child, she's alive and kicking—emphatically kicking," he said grimly.

"How do you know?" she asked in astonishment.

"Also, you are reported dead," John went on, looking at her thoughtfully. "The motor-boat was picked up in mid-ocean—in other words, twenty-five miles from Spithead —and I presume Mrs. Dorban has told some story about an accident which threw you both into the water. There is no mystery about my having this knowledge," he smiled. "We have had a very full radio description of the tragedy. The only thing that puzzles me is why the dickens did she try to kill you?"

Pen was silent on this subject.

"Do you discuss these matters with the captain?" she asked.

"You are being sarcastic again," said John wearily. "Sarcasm always rattles me. No, but we poor, humble sailors learn a lot by keeping our ears open."

He made no further remark but went out, and later Penelope saw him on the deck polishing the brasswork in that leisurely, detached way which sailors have when they are engaged in routine labour.

He was dressed lightly in trousers and undershirt; the weather had changed, as he had predicted, and it was hot on deck, for they had a following wind behind them.

He wore a short-sleeved singlet, and from her place of observation she could admire the patent strength in the brown, muscular arm. Presently he put his cleaning rags into a tin case and disappeared from view.

She walked forward after him and, looking into the well, saw the inevitable Hollin with his no less inevitable cigar, but John had disappeared, and she felt unaccountably annoyed.

Mr. Orford was asleep under his umbrella, Bobby was squatting on the deck playing solitaire, Dr. Fraser, that dour man, was reading a fat and uninteresting book. Nobody spoke to her. The doctor looked up as she passed ; an officer, whom she took to be the mate of the ship, deliberately avoided her, and for the first time she felt very lonely.

Half an hour later she paced to the further end of the ship, and, looking over the rail, she beheld an extraordinary sight.

John was sitting on a stool, and on his knee was a large paint-box, the lid of which

served as an easel; inside had been fastened
a small canvas, which he was busy covering
with paint. She watched fascinated, and saw
the grey-green of the sea, the gold and eau-
de-nil of the westerly sky, appear under his
nimble brush.

He had perched himself on the top of
the fore-hatch, so that he enjoyed an un-
interrupted view of the sea, and he was so
absorbed with his work that he did not
notice the girl until her shadow fell across
him, then he started guiltily and looked up.

"Y-yes," he said, answering her ecstatic
gasp of delight. "It isn't bad for a ten-
minute sketch."

"But you are an artist, John! Whatever——"

He put down his brushes and closed the
box hurriedly.

"An amateur, a mere dabbler. The poor
must have their pleasures," he said glibly,
"as well as the rich, and——"

"Hi!"

There was a bellow of sound from the deck above, and, looking up, Penelope saw Mr. Orford, and for once his equanimity was disturbed.

" Say, what in thunder were you doing— painting—you great boob—didn't I tell you —oh, you poor fish!"

Mr. Orford was really angry.

John flushed a deep red, but, to her surprise, made no reply, as the fat man came wobbling down the companion-way. The sailor looked for all the world like a sheepish boy who had been detected in a forbidden orchard.

" I told you not to paint!" said Mr. Orford furiously. "I told you that you weren't— oh, what in hell's the use!"

"I am very sorry, Mr. Orford," said John humbly. " It was a thoughtless thing to do."

Mr. Orford flung out his plump hands in a gesture of despair.

" Sump 'n's got to happen," he said darkly.

"Never in all my experience have things gone worse!"

Rumbling his wrath, he climbed breathlessly to the deck and disappeared, and John looked at the girl with a gleam of amusement in his fine eyes.

"You see what you've done for me," he said.

"What I've done!" she said indignantly. "*I* haven't been painting. But I think it is disgraceful that you aren't allowed to amuse yourself in your spare time if you want to paint."

"I have no spare time," said the other with a little grimace. "I am on duty for twenty-four hours. Excuse me, I must placate what Carlyle would call the enraged mountain."

The sun had touched the horizon when, looking far out to sea, to the south, Penelope saw a ship. It seemed to be heading straight in their direction. Glancing aft, she saw a

little group, consisting of Mr. Orford, the
captain, and Bobby Mills, engaged in an
earnest confabulation. Presently the doctor
joined them, and from time to time they
looked toward the oncoming steamer. Suddenly the doctor detached himself from the
group and came toward her.

"Good-afternoon, Miss Pitt," he said,
eyeing her steadily. "You don't seem very
well."

He did not seem very well himself. His
face had paled, his hands were shaking.

"I?" she said in amazement. "I am as
well as ever I have been."

"I don't think you are very well. A touch
of sun, I should imagine." He looked into
her eyes. "Yes, off you go to bed."

She stared at him.

"But really I am very well, doctor."

"That is an illusion," said he, pleasantly
for him. "Will you please do as I tell you."

"But—really—to bed?"

He nodded.

"When you are in bed I will come and see you and give you a cooling drink."

"But it is ridiculous!" she said rebelliously. "I don't see why I should go to bed when I feel——"

"Will you do as you are told, Miss Pitt?" This time his voice was stern and uncompromising, and she realized that her health had nothing whatever to do with his strange request.

To stand out against his wishes was impossible. She was at the mercy of these men, and yet she did not fear them.

"Very well," she said. "I think it is wholly unnecessary, but if you say I must, I will."

Lying in bed, the absurdity of the situation dawned upon her, and she was amused, though she was more angry.

The doctor came in with a medicine measure in his hand; it was half-filled with a cloudy white liquid.

"Drink this," he said.

"But, seriously, doctor, do you think I have sunstroke? I assure you my head was never clearer."

"Drink this," he said again, and she obeyed.

It was a bitter draught, and she made a grimace as she swallowed.

"Ugh!" she said, and for the first time since they had met, the doctor smiled.

"Not pleasant, eh? Still, its effects are very pleasant indeed, and its after effects are nil. That is the big advantage of this potion."

His voice seemed very far away, and Penelope was experiencing a delicious sense of languorous ease.

IT was quite dark when she woke. The ship was still on the way and no lights were burning in the cabin. Reaching out her hand, she switched on the bedside lamp and sat up. Her head felt curiously light, but did not ache. But when she put her feet to the ground her knees wobbled for a second.

Then the doctor had been right, she thought.

"Mercy!" said Penelope aloud, for she had caught the reflection of her face in the wardrobe glass. It was covered with pink spots—forehead, chin, neck, all bore that tell-tale rash.

"Measles!" She had recognized the symptoms with a groan, and went back to bed.

When she opened her eyes again it was daylight; a gentle tap at the door had awakened her.

"Put it down, John," she said; "and don't please come near; I have measles."

The door opened a few inches, a long, sinewy arm came in and deposited a tray, and then John's voice said :

"Try soap and water."

"Try what?" she repeated incredulously.

"Soap and water," said John soothingly. "It is the finest remedy for measles the world has ever known. I am thinking of patenting the cure."

He had hardly closed the door before she was out of bed and in the bathroom, applying a wet sponge vigorously to her face. And the spots came off! She could hardly believe her eyes, and yet it was true. Under the vigorous application of a damp sponge her face was cleared of the rash.

The first person she saw when she stepped

out on to the deck that morning was John. He was sitting in a shady corner, and he was engaged in the prosaic business of peeling potatoes. It is not customary for the mysteries of the cook's department to be revealed upon that part of the yacht which is reserved for the expensive pleasures of guests, but by now Penelope had grown accustomed to the inexplicable, and had she seen John sitting on the edge of the funnel drinking champagne, it would not have been more remarkable than some of the sights she had witnessed since she had been an unwelcome member of Mr. Orford's party.

At the sight of her, he put down his knife and a half-peeled potato, and rose, wiping his hands upon his jersey.

"A messy business," he said, "but I am not allowed to carry a handkerchief, for fear of exciting the envy of the crew."

She glanced round. There was nobody in sight, except one of the deck hands who was splicing a rope at the far end of the promenade-deck.

"Now, John, you've got to tell me—how did those spots come on my face?"

"'Open confession is good for the soul,'" replied John. "I painted them!"

"You painted them?" she gasped.

He nodded.

"You have already had proof of my artistic qualities," he said, "so you may be sure that the work was well carried out. The unfortunate thing is that we couldn't wash them off without waking you."

"Then I was drugged?" she said.

He hesitated.

"I was drugged?" she repeated.

"You were given a sleeping draught, I understand," said John carefully. "It was against my wish, but Orford insisted. You see," he went on, "we came upon a British warship which ordered us to stop, and as we desired the stay of their examining officers should be a very short one, we hoisted the yellow jack to show we had an infectious disease on board—and you were the infectious disease."

"Was there no other reason?"

He did not reply for a moment. Then:

"Possibly Mr. Orford thought that you might describe our stealthy habits. Anyway, it was an unpleasant business, and I am glad it is all over."

She shook her head helplessly.

"I can't understand it," she said.

"But you are not frightened?" he asked, looking at her keenly.

"No, I am not frightened," she admitted. "I am just very much annoyed."

"That's all right," he said, and it seemed that he was relieved. "And now I am going to give you a piece of information. The ship is going into Vigo. Something has happened to one of the engines. I don't know what it is, because I am not an engineer. But we are going into Vigo for two or three days, and you will have an opportunity of buying clothes."

"Shall I be allowed ashore?"

"Under escort," he said gravely; "and I have agreed to act as your escort. In a way your coming on board was providential; it may even be miraculous," he went on, seriously enough. "I don't know—it may be—it depends entirely upon you. And— here comes the jolly old Bobby and I return to my potatoes."

Bobby was certainly more jolly-looking than he had been during the past few days.

"Has John told you about your measles?" he said. "Can you ever forgive us, Miss Pitt? It was a blackguardly thing to do, and it took all our persuasive powers to induce the doctor to help in this nefarious scheme. He hasn't stopped telling us that he is liable to imprisonment for seven years, to be struck off the Medical Register, and ruined for life."

"Then why did he do it?" asked Pen a little frigidly.

"Because the Frasers have always helped the Campbells in time of trouble. Not that the Campbells are involved in this transaction, but Fraser's a kinsman of ours, and that explains the sacrifice of professional dignity. You are going to forgive us, aren't you, Miss Pitt?"

"I don't see what difference my forgiveness would make," she said, half smiling. "I wish you'd have told me, and I should have been happy to have acted the part of an interesting invalid."

"That wasn't all that was required," said Bobby very gravely, and then: "You know we are going into Vigo?"

She nodded.

"John told you; he is a talkative bird; I suppose it is because——"

"Because?"

"Oh, well, men are born gossips." he said lamely.

CERTAIN amazing facts were slowly emerging through the fog which enveloped Penelope's mind. Perhaps that is hardly an accurate description. It was rather as though, from the moment Cynthia had called her to the house, she had been under the influence of an anæsthetic, in which condition the most fantastic happenings seemed natural. Now the effect of the drug was wearing away, and she was examining, incredulously, events which she had been satisfied to accept as being perfectly normal and logical.

Piecing her chaotic experiences together, she arrived definitely at this point—that Cynthia Dorban had set out in cold blood to murder her, for no other reason, apparently, than because she had opened a trunk which contained a large amount of money and two etchings. It seemed an inadequate cause. But obviously the deadly secret of Stone House was in that trunk, which Cynthia had thought had been sunk in the sea. Why should she want to destroy an immense fortune, was not the least of the mysteries. Cynthia was a woman who lived for money. It was the one subject on which she could become interesting, and however a conversation might start, it invariably came back, by some channel or other, to the solid matter of hard cash.

In the early morning, as the *Polyantha* was making for the rugged, blue coast-line of Spain, Penelope got out of bed and, wrapped in a dressing-gown, went on to the deck.

Early as was the hour, she found a fellow-passenger in Mr. Orford, who, to her surprise, was fully dressed.

The morning was chilly, and he was wrapped in a huge greatcoat, the collar of which was turned up about his ears, and with his hands thrust into his pockets he surveyed the approaching land with a scowl of gloom.

He started violently at her voice—she was wearing her slippers and he had not heard her approach—and half-turned as though he were going to beat a retreat.

"Up early, eh, Miss Pitt?"

She thought he looked at her with a very unfavourable eye, and this suspicion of hostility was confirmed when, with a simultaneous jerk of his thumb and head toward the approaching land, he blurted:

"Your idea?"

"My idea?" she said in astonishment. "Why, I don't quite know what you mean, Mr. Orford."

"When sentiment comes into organization, organization gets sick," he said bitterly. "Thought it was you; perhaps I'm wrong. Perhaps it is the other thing; and yet I'm supposed to be in charge!"

She could only look at him. To her he

was incoherent, wild of speech, and beyond understanding.

"Going into Vigo is madness," he said helplessly, shrugging his vast shoulders. "Say, I've known men to be taken to the insane asylum for less."

"But I thought the engines were wrong," she began.

"Engines wrong?" he boomed. "There's nothin' wrong with *Polyantha*. Fasten that fact to your mind. *Polyantha* was never better. No, sir. There is sump 'n wrong, but not with *Polyantha*. It is in that crazy man's mind; that's what's wrong," he said heatedly. "Six months' organization, and" —he snapped his fingers—"and all because——" He looked at her from under his heavy brows. "Or maybe it isn't you at all." He turned abruptly away and stalked down the deck, she staring after him.

And she had been in a mind to tell him the whole truth about Cynthia Dorban. She had wakened thinking about Stone House and the mystery of the trunk, and at the sight of him there came an urge within her to find a confidant. Mr. Orford was not in the mood for confidences.

It was nine o'clock when the *Polyantha* came to her moorings in Vigo Harbour, and in the early morning sunlight the town looked ethereally pretty, with its background of mountainous hills. It was less beautiful at close quarters, she was to find. A tiny motor-boat had been lowered away, and into this she was handed by the faithful John. In honour of the occasion he had made himself look spruce. His somewhat ill-fitting clothes were new, and his flat-brimmed hat, with its ribbon inscribed in gold letters with the word *Polyantha*, might have been more imposing if it had not been a size too small.

They had passed through the Customs and were walking up the narrow street toward the Calle Principe when she asked :

"Why did you tell me that the engines wanted repair?"

" Don't they ? " he asked in mock surprise.

" You know very well they do not," she said severely. " You are in Mr. Mills' secrets. Why did he bring the *Polyantha* into Vigo ? Mr. Orford thought at first I was the cause."

" I think you do Bobby an injustice," said John quietly. " He had a very special reason for visiting Vigo, if it is true that the story of engine trouble is an invention. Here is the principal thoroughfare "—he silenced any further comment she might make— " and you will be able to buy anything you want."

Suddenly she realized that she was penniless and laughed.

" Unfortunately," she said dryly, " I am not sufficiently well-known to the shop-keepers in Vigo."

" Haven't you any money ? " he asked quickly. " Of course, you haven't." He put his hand in his pocket and took out a flat note-case and extracted a dozen Spanish

6

bills. "How careless of me! Mr. Mills gave me this in case you had no—what a fool I am!"

She hesitated before she took the money. "One of these will be enough. How much is a thousand pesetas?"

"Roughly forty pounds, and forty pounds is two hundred dollars," he said rapidly. "You'll find me waiting at the corner. I think that shop over there—Manuels—sell the best woman's truck, but if you can't find what you want there, there is rather a nice little store round the corner, facing the cathedral."

It was not a moment to argue. She crossed the square to the famous Manuels and made her purchases. It was surprising the number of things she had to buy—the more surprising that she had not felt the need of them until she confronted them, ticketed unintelligibly. She bought two cheap dresses and a respectable quantity of other mysteries, and came out laden, to find the patient John standing by the side of a fiacre which he had hired.

He took the parcels from her hands and stowed them neatly.

"I am afraid I have spent a terrible lot of money," she began, but he shook his head.

"Bobby expected you would; and anyway, a thousand pesetas is not a terrifying sum."

He looked at her thoughtfully.

"I wonder if you will come with me for a little drive?" he asked. "I have a call to make."

"Do you know Vigo?" she asked in surprise.

He nodded.

"Very well indeed," he replied quietly. "I am going now to——" He seemed in doubt as to whether he should proceed, and then: "To the cemetery. Do you mind, Miss Pitt?"

"Not at all," she said in haste. She wondered no more. Some friend of his must be buried in this out-of-the-way spot, but it could hardly have been the sentimentality of John the steward which had brought the *Polyantha* into Vigo.

As they drove through the crowded streets he pointed out various places of interest.

"Vigo is not particularly well endowed in the matter of historical monuments," he said. "Most of the cathedrals in this part of the country were injured in an earthquake, and restored in a most ghastly modern fashion."

He told her that somewhere at the bottom of the sea, in Vigo Harbour, lay a million pounds' worth of silver; that it was here that one of the old English admirals surprised the Spanish Silver Fleet, sank half of the ships and captured the others.

They came at last to the cemetery, which stood on the outskirts of the town, a great square desolation of garish iron crosses and horrible metal wreaths, enclosed within a high and ugly wall.

An old gate-keeper came forward to meet him, looking at him curiously, and John addressed him in fluent Spanish. The old man leading the way, they threaded a narrow path and came presently to a corner of the cemetery railed off from the remainder.

"This is the English burying ground, Miss Pitt," explained John, "though in point of fact there are more Americans here than there are British."

The little corner was carefully kept. There were flowers everywhere, and the crosses and headstones were less ornate than those in the larger cemetery.

"Will you excuse me?" His voice was low, the face, at which she flashed a quick look, was set as in a mask.

She knew he wanted to be alone, and nodded.

Walking forward a few paces, he came to the side of a grave which bore a single stone at its head. Stooping, he picked off the dead leaves of a rose bush which grew by its side, and then, bareheaded, he stood at the foot motionless, his head bent, his eyes fixed upon the ground.

Presently he looked round and beckoned her forward.

"I didn't intend bringing you in," he said. "I had almost forgotten your presence until you were here. This is my mother's grave," he said simply.

She looked at the headstone and read:

"Mary Tyson" (she could not read the other word), aged 46. Third daughter of Lord John Medway."

He stooped again, and selecting a rose, twisted it from its stem and laid it carefully upon the grassy mound; then, without another word, he took her arm and led her back to the gate.

They were in town again before he explained.

"We lived here for very many years. My father was poor, and the climate of Vigo suited him very well. I scarcely remember him; I was about six or seven when he died. Mother and I lived here for twelve years."

They were passing through the Calle de

Principe when he rose, and, leaning over the driver, gave a direction, and the cab turned down a long and narrow street. At a word the cab stopped before a small shop.

"This is where we lived," said John, and pointed up. "On the second floor. It seems empty now. I wonder if old Gonsalez is still alive."

He got down on to the sidewalk and peered through the window, and, opening the door of the shop, went in. He came back in a few minutes.

"The old man died four years ago," he said, and exhibited a large key. "But I have permission to look over the house. The rooms are empty. Old Gonsalez was devoted to dear mother, and swore he would never let the rooms once we had gone, and the old boy has kept his promise."

He inserted the key in a side door, and she followed him along a long and narrow passage, and up a particularly steep and narrow winding stairway.

"Here we are," said John.

The landing on which they stopped was lit only by a small window.

"This was our dining-room," he said, and opened the door.

The room was empty and dusty, cobwebs hung in the corners, and a tiny charcoal grate was half-hidden by an accumulation of rubbish, but the walls were panelled in carved oak, and the ceiling, despite its dust and discoloration, was a beautiful piece of plaster-work.

"Moorish," explained John. "The house was originally built by a Malaga merchant, who brought Moorish workmen to decorate the ceilings."

He led her from room to room, stopping now and again to indicate some particular object which his memory associated with his mother.

It did not occur to her that he was presuming a great deal upon her interest in his early life. She was interested, profoundly interested.

"Now if you can find your way down alone," said John, "I'm going to sit here for five minutes and have a real think. I want to get certain things straight in my mind, and I don't know any atmosphere more conducive to clear thinking than these dear rooms."

She nodded, and, understanding, went quietly away.

She had reached the first flight and her foot was on the stair to descend to the ground floor, when she heard voices in the hall below. Somebody was speaking in broken English.

"You may see them; yes, they are very nice rooms, but at the moment there is a gentleman and lady to inspect. My father would never hire these rooms, but with me it is different. These are hard times and a man must win money."

"Certainly," said a second voice, and Penelope drew back with a gasp. She recognized it instantly; it was the voice of Arthur Dorban!

6*

"Shall we go up?" It was Cynthia speaking, and the girl reeled back against the ancient balustrade.

Before they could move a step, she was flying up the stairs and had rushed into the room where John was sitting on the broad window-ledge, his hands clasped about a bent knee, his head sunk in thought. He looked up quickly at the sound of her hurrying feet.

"Somebody downstairs—I don't wish to see them."

"Who?"

"Mr. and—Mrs. Dorban!"

He uttered an exclamation.

"Dorban here?" He ran to the door, opened it, and stood on the landing listening to the sound of ascending footsteps, and then, beckoning her silently, went up a third flight of stairs to the landing above.

"Don't make a sound," he whispered. "Keep flat against the wall."

Cynthia's voice came up to them.

"But why should he come to this poky

little hole, Arthur?" she asked petulantly.
"And how could he get here?"

"There are many reasons why he should
come, and many ways he could come," said
Arthur. "I'll stake my life that I'm not
wrong. There was a yacht came in this
morning, too; I'm going to have a look at
her."

"Excuse me," said the Spaniard's voice,
"I will tell the lady and gentleman that
you are here."

Apparently they were on the landing
below, for they heard the feet of the land-
lord go into the room. He came out in a
few minutes.

"They've gone," he said, in a tone of indignation. "Also the key which I told the
sailor to return."

"The sailor?" interrupted Arthur Dorban
sharply. "Which sailor was that?"

Apparently they all went into the room
together. John, stretching his head cautiously
forward, saw that the landing was empty.

"Now!" he said.

In two seconds they were on the landing and racing down the lower flight. They heard voices above and hurrying footsteps as John slammed the street door and turned the key in the lock. He said something in Spanish to the driver, and the fiacre literally flew along the streets at a breakneck pace to the little quay. The driver had hardly jerked his steaming horse to a halt before John was out and flinging the parcels down into the little boat that was moored to the quayside.

He pushed a Spanish note in the man's hand, ran down the slimy steps, and almost lifted the girl into the boat. As they went at full speed across the harbour, he looked back from time to time, and presently saw what he had been expecting. A second fiacre joined the first, and the girl recognized the man who jumped out.

"Is that Arthur Dorban?" asked John.

She nodded.

"I should have liked a closer inspection of the gentleman," said John thoughtfully, and then after a pause : "I rather fancy we have made a mess of poor old Orford's organization." He chuckled softly, though for him it was no laughing matter.

The boat drew alongside of the yacht, and the girl ran up the gangway before him.

A gloomy group, consisting of Bobby, the captain, and James Xenocrates Orford, were awaiting their arrival.

"We have had an unfortunate meeting in the town," said John without preliminary.

"Not Dorban?" exploded Mr. Orford.

John nodded.

"Yes, I didn't see him, but Miss Pitt saw him, and at this precise moment he is looking for a boatman to bring him out to the *Polyantha;* so I think on the whole," said John carefully, "it would be an excellent idea if we got out of this harbour p.d.q."

"Oh, you do, do you?" rasped Mr. Orford, with an attempt at a sneer. "Well, I'd like to ask you whether you are prepared to go without Hollin?"

"Without Hollin?" gasped John.

Mr. Orford nodded.

"Without Hollin, I repeat," said Mr. Orford. "He left the ship five minutes after you, and rowed himself ashore in a dinghy. We didn't see the lil' angel till he was nearing land, and if by this time he is not uproariously drunk and shooting up Vigo, I shall be a much surprised and happy man."

They looked at one another in consternation, and it was left to the captain to supply a suggestion.

"I'd better get up anchor and stand out to sea," he said. "We can send a couple of men in the motor-boat back as soon as it gets dark, to pick up Hollin; obviously he cannot be left."

"And then?" asked Mr. Orford darkly.

The old captain shrugged his shoulders.

Bobby left the group and went aft, taking on his way a telescope from a bracket. He focussed the glass upon the shore, and made a long and earnest scrutiny of a gesticulating little group he saw on the quayside.

The captain was making his way to the bridge when he turned.

"One moment, Captain Willit," he said. "I think this little trouble will work itself out. Our precipitous friends are coming aboard."

Orford uttered an exclamation of surprise, and, seizing the telescope from Bobby's hand, scrutinized the foreshore. Then he drew a long sigh.

"The Lord hath delivered them into our hands," he said piously. "Your sheep are surely advancing to the fold, Willit."

"My sheep?" said the puzzled captain.

"There's an old saying that you might as well be hung for a sheep as a goat," said Mr. Orford, "and that old he-goat being definitely and completely dead, there is no real reason why the sheep shouldn't become mutton."

A quarter of an hour's hard rowing by the one perspiring boatman brought Cynthia Dorban and her husband alongside the gangway.

"The captain, sir?" said the innocent deck hand who received them. "Yes, sir, you can see the captain. Will you come aboard?"

For answer Cynthia grasped the outstretched hand, and swung herself on to the grating, but Mr. Dorban did not immediately follow.

"Do you think you are wise, Cynthia?" he said. "Suppose he is on board?"

Cynthia's thin lips curled.

"The only fear I have is that he isn't," she said significantly, and with some reluctance he followed.

Cynthia had never seen Mr. Orford before, and at the sight of that benevolent man, with a yachting cap rakishly pulled over his right eye, and a large cigar in the corner of his mouth, she was a little puzzled, for Mr. James Xenocrates Orford diffused, by his very presence, an atmosphere of opulence and innocence.

" Are you the captain?" said Cynthia with her sweetest smile.

"Why, no, I am not the captain," said Mr. Orford, to whom a falsehood was repugnant; " I am the owner."

" Then you will be able to help me more than the captain," said Cynthia. " This is my husband, Mr. Arthur Dorban, and we have reason to believe that a man on board this ship—quite unknown to you——" And then she stopped dead, and for a moment her self-possession deserted her. Looking aft, she saw a girl sitting in a deck-chair, her eyes fixed upon the visitors.

" My God !" whispered Cynthia. " Arthur, look !"

Slico's face turned an unhealthy yellow.

" Get out of this," he said under his breath, and turned to go, but the sailor on the gangway barred all egress.

And then Mr. Orford's gentle voice

brought the couple to a realization of their unhappy position.

"Sump'n tells me you're going to behave," said Mr. Orford gently. "I'd hate a rough-house right here in the harbour of a presum'bly friendly nation."

There was no kindness in his eyes now.

"If you go through that door on the left and down the companion-way, I'll come and talk with you," said Mr. Orford persuasively. "An' if you make a fuss, I've gotta hurt you, though it is repellent to my finest feelings. Now step lively!" His custardy voice became suddenly a menacing bark.

Arthur Dorban was the first to recognize the inevitability of the situation, and without a word turned into the deck-house and passed down the companion-way to the saloon.

His wife followed, a little dazed.

Mr. Orford shut the rosewood door of the saloon and motioned his uncomfortable guests to be seated.

"Let's get this thing right, Mr. Dorban," he said. "You are here looking for somebody, and that somebody is on board. I guess there is another somebody that you didn't expect to see, but she's an accident."

"I suppose you know that this is an act of piracy, and that you can be——"

Mr. Orford interrupted Arthur Dorban's protest with a lofty gesture.

"It is such a long time since I was a law-abiding member of society that I hardly know what it feels like," he said. "Yes, sir, I am well aware that I am breaking three distinct and separate laws, but what's a law more or less?"

"Will you tell me what you intend doing with us?" asked Cynthia, who was very pale.

"I'm just asking you to be a member of my little yachting-party; we are now on our way to the South Sea Islands," said Mr. Orford. "I'm going to give you my own cabin, and I freely confess that I hate turning out of it; it is one of the two private suites on the *Polyantha*, and luxury is my weakness."

"I don't suppose you imagine for one moment that our disappearance will not create any suspicion," said Arthur Dorban. "I have already notified the police as to the object of my visit, and the British Vice-Consul——"

"You have notified nobody," said Mr. Orford, still gently. "You haven't had time, for your train only arrived at eleven o'clock, and it is now twelve. I was thinking it out while I came down the companion-way. It took you a day to get to London, and you came from Paris to Madrid—you couldn't have done it under unless you came by aeroplane. There's a train leaves Madrid for Vigo early in the morning, but you couldn't have connected with that, not even if you had made the change at Valladolid. There used to be a connection at Valladolid," said Mr. Orford reminiscently; "you could change at four o'clock in the morning, if your train was on time, and get a connection through to Vigo, but they knocked off that train during the war. You could have got a connection through Corunna, but that would have brought you through to Vigo at two o'clock in the afternoon. No, sir, you've seen nobody, and that bluff doesn't pay dividend."

"What are you going to do with us?" asked Cynthia again.

"I am going to keep you in that cabin, and if you behave you'll have a bully time. If you don't behave——" He shook his head mournfully, as though the mere contemplation of the consequence was painful to him.

In the meantime John was interviewing the patient boatman, who, hooked to the gangway of *Polyantha*, was waiting for the return of his fares.

"The señor sends you this," said John in Spanish. "He is staying to lunch."

"Perhaps if I return, señor sailor?" suggested the boatman happily, for the fee which

John had handed him was a generous one, and the promise of its repetition filled the boatman's soul with happiness.

"We ourselves will put the señor ashore," said John gravely, but he did not say where.

The boatman rode off content.

A search party went ashore charged with the double duty of looking up Mr. Hollin and bringing the Dorbans' trunks on board. It was the practical Cynthia who had suggested this, and in confessing, as she did, that they were waiting at the station, she confirmed Orford's theories.

"There is no sense in going on this beastly voyage without clothes," she said to her husband in the privacy of their cabin, which was all that Xenocrates Orford had claimed it. "Did they search you?"

He nodded.

"They found nothing," he said. "I had time to push the gun under the sofa. Even Orford, who was looking on, didn't see it go. And you?"

"They looked into my handbag and found the baggage checks," she said. "There was nothing else to find. Arthur, he is on board."

"Of course he is on board," said Arthur Dorban irritably. "You don't imagine they'd take this step if he wasn't, do you? I knew you were a fool to leave the boat. We've walked blindly into the most palpable trap——"

But Cynthia Dorban was not listening to his reproaches. The presence of Penelope Pitt on board had shocked her. She was satisfied in her mind that Penelope was dead, and the sight of her very much alive and on the *Polyantha*, of all places, probably associating with the one man in the world who it was fatal for Cynthia's plan that she should meet, had almost made her swoon.

"What is she doing here?" asked Arthur Dorban, coming to the subject of her thoughts.

"God knows," said Mrs. Dorban. "It is the most tragic coincidence."

Arthur pulled at his little black moustache.

"Do you think she knows?"

"Do you think they would be running away from us if she did know?" snapped his wife. "And there is no mystery about her being on board; she must have been picked up at sea. That explains why the *Princess* was empty when it was found—but to be picked up by him!"

Cynthia sat on the broad divan, her knees drawn, her hands clasped above them, and her pretty face was wrinkled in thought.

"I don't think it could have happened better," she said at last.

Arthur Dorban was unpacking his trunk, and he looked round in surprise.

"What the devil do you mean?" he demanded.

"Our being on this ship with Penelope and this man. Bobby Mills is here, naturally; but who is the fat man?"

Suddenly Dorban straightened his back from his task, looked at her, and whistled.

"Hollin!" he said. "He would be here, of course. Do you remember what they told us in London about Hollin? If that is true——"

She nodded.

"I was thinking about Hollin," she said slowly. "Don't you see, Arthur, that if Hollin is the kind of man they say he is, how providential it might be—— Where did you put your pistol?"

He pulled it out from beneath the sofa, and she took it in her hand and, raising her dress, slipped it into a pocket of her under-skirt.

"Yes, it is all for the best," she said.

Mr. Hollin had had a thoroughly enjoyable day. He had started well by discovering Mr. Orford's pocket-case in his cabin. In the excitement of anchoring, and when the stout man had been on the deck, more worried than interested in the forthcoming shore-trip of Penelope Pitt and her escort, Hollin had made a very careful examination of the big man's cabin, and the result had been eminently satisfactory, for in the pocket-book were twenty five-pound bank-notes. A dinghy that had been lowered in case of emergency supplied Mr. Hollin with the opportunity for leaving the ship, and all that followed was natural and inevitable. He changed twenty pounds into Spanish money, and became, in consequence, the Grand Master of Vigo.

Once he had seen John and the girl driving

through the Grand Place, and had gone to cover.

By two o'clock in the afternoon Mr. Hollin was completely drunk, and was sleeping off his early indiscretion in the back room of a small wine shop, the proprietor of which was well satisfied to retain on the premises one whose fabulous wealth gave promise of a profitable evening.

It was nearing sunset when he woke, with a colossal thirst. A bottle of white wine that had the flavour of pinewood brought him to an agreeable frame of mind. He could not speak Spanish, but found that no handicap, and he swaggered into the darkening streets, his hands in his pockets, his coarse face aflame; and in the thing he called his heart, a desire for adventure.

He fell in with a guide—one of those pestiferous individuals who are to be found in every Continental town. He spoke English with a Manchester accent, and Mr. Hollin hailed him as a friend.

"You are the fellow I have been waiting to see all day," he said. "Show me the sights. I have got plenty of money—anywhere there is dancing and girls—women are my weakness."

He fetched up in a low quarter of the town at a little *fonda*, where men strum on guitars and scantily attired ladies dance Spanish dances which were popular in a less enlightened and more indelicate age. Mr. Hollin, in his glory, was sitting at a table strewn with bottles of Rioja, indifferent whisky, and cheap champagne, with a girl on each knee, and he was singing at the top of his voice a sentimental ballad about his "old-fashioned mother," when there approached him one who was obviously not Spanish—a tall, middle-aged man, the very erectness of whom would have warned Mr. Hollin, if he had been in a less genial mood.

"Are you English?" asked the stranger, pulling a chair to the table.

" That's me, mate, I'm English. Orstralian to be exact. Have a drink?"

The stranger poured himself out a modest quantity from a bottle which was at least labelled " Whisky," and diluted the poison plentifully.

"What is your ship?" asked the stranger carelessly.

"Ship?" Mr. Hollin frowned. "What do you mean—'ship'?"

" You're a sailor, aren't you? Only sailors come to Vigo," said the stranger.

" I am and I'm not," hiccupped Mr. Hollin gravely. "I'm a sailor, but I'm a passenger. Who are you, anyway?" he asked with sudden truculence.

"Oh, I'm just a—traveller."

"Well, travel," said Hollin loudly, his suspicions aroused. "Don't try and pry into my business, because I regard that as a liberty."

"I'm sorry," said the other with a quiet smile. "Here's luck!"

He sipped at his drink, and a mollified Mr. Hollin advanced further information about himself.

It was inaccurate, and not very ingenious, and presently his guest made an excuse and went back to his table. The guide leant forward and brought the drunkard's attention away from the lady into whose eyes he was gazing.

"That man is an English detective," he whispered, and instantly Mr. Hollin was very sober.

"How do you know?"

"He came this morning. One of my friends has been translating for him," said the guide.

Through Hollin's fuddled brain ran a shiver of apprehension.

"A detective?" he said uneasily. "What's he doing here?"

"I don't know; he's looking for a man— he has been making some inquiries about

some English people who used to live in
Vigo. He has been here several days."

Hollin rubbed his unshaven chin and
blinked near-sightedly across the smoky
room to where the tall man sat, apparently
immersed in the *Heraldo de Madrid.*

"Here, matey," he lowered his voice,
"find out what's his name. I've an idea I
know him."

"It is a curious name—Spinner."

"Hell!" gasped Hollin. "I thought I
knew him!"

He was completely sober now, alert so far
as his slow brain permitted, very much on
his guard. He sipped the long glass of wine,
and then, beckoning the waiter furtively,
paid his score, and lurched out of the wine
shop with his guide. Glancing back out of
the corner of his eye, he saw the detective
had risen and was following.

"Here, take this," said Hollin, and thrust
a note into the guide's hand. "Keep that

fellow in conversation, Johnny; I've got to see a friend."

He raced down the darkened street, blundering wildly into side turnings, in an endeavour to reach the main thoroughfare. For a quarter of an hour he was lost in a labyrinth of streets, and since he knew no Spanish, and could not even frame a question as to the nearest way to the quay where he had left his boat, he had to find his way without assistance.

It was half an hour before he emerged through the mouth of a crooked street to a view of the sea.

He came to the quay—not a soul was in sight. Peering down the stone steps, he saw his little boat dancing with the tide, and heaved a deep sigh of relief.

His foot was on the steps when somebody touched his shoulder, and such were the state of his nerves that he uttered a frightened exclamation.

" It is all right."

Instantly he recognized the voice. It was the detective.

"I was waiting to have a talk with you," said Mr. Spinner. "Maybe you didn't see me."

"I didn't," said Hollin, breathing through his nose. "Anyway, I'm busy; I've got to get out to my ship?"

"Which is your ship?" asked the other carelessly.

"The *Moss Rose*," said Hollin glibly. "From Swansea—that's a port in Wales."

It was the only ship's name he knew. It was less of a ship than a pleasure yacht that plied for hire at a well-known South Coast resort which Mr. Hollin had once visited for business purposes.

"*Moss Rose*, eh?" said Spinner thoughtfully. "I didn't know she was in the harbour."

Hollin made to pass the man.

"I can't stop," said he. "The captain told me to be on board——"

7

But a firm hand gripped his arm and drew him back to the quayside.

"You know me. I'm Spinner of Scotland Yard. Your name is Hollin."

"My name is Jackson," said Hollin loudly. "I don't know anything about Scotland Yard."

"Your name is Hollin and I am going to take you to the Spanish police station," said the patient Spinner; and then : "Where is your pal?" he wheedled. "What is the good of making a fuss? You are a sensible man, and I'll see that you are treated right."

"My name is Jackson," said the other doggedly, and tried to pull.

A whistle shrilled and instantly the quay seemed alive with policemen. Mr. Hollin, recognizing the inevitability, accepted his fate with such philosophy as he was capable of expressing.

"This is your man, sergeant," said Spinner, speaking in Spanish. "Just hold him while I go down and have a look at that rowboat he was making for; it is pretty certain to have the name of his ship upon it."

There was a surprise in store for Mr. Spinner. The boat which had been lying at the foot of the steps, which he had seen, but had not had time to examine before the arrival of Hollin, was now adrift, and was apparently floating empty to the centre of the harbour. Spinner was puzzled. The man had not had time to cast off the painter, and he could have sworn that the boat was firmly secured when the arrest had been made. Yet there it was, dimly to be seen in the darkness, a bobbing blur and empty. In that light he could not see the man who was lying full length across the seat, using his hands as paddles.

Spinner did not trouble to make any attempt to secure the boat; that could be picked up by the local police, and he made a request to this effect.

With curiously uncomfortable handcuffs

about his wrists, Hollin was hustled into a fiacre and driven back through the town, inwardly cursing himself for the folly which had entangled him in a moment when he was dreaming of the luxury and freedom which a Southern American State would have offered him.

Without the usual preliminary interrogation with which he was familiar, Hollin was hurried through the back of the police premises to a long one-storied building; a steel gate was open, and he was thrust into a large, unlighted room, and the grille clanged upon him.

"THEY'VE got Hollin," said John. His voice was quiet, unemotional. He might have been passing on an item of casual news.

"Oh, they've got him, have they?" said Mr. Orford.

In her heart Penelope Pitt was glad to hear the news. She could not immediately recognize the significance or what effect this arrest might have upon her. Somehow she knew it was an arrest; she had always thought of Hollin as a criminal character who, for some reason, Bobby Mills was trying to spirit away from England.

They were sitting—Orford, Bobby, and she—on the after-deck, when the tall figure of John appeared out of the gloom, to make his simple but momentous pronouncement.

"'Shall we fight or shall we fly? Good

Sir Richard, tell me now,'" Bobby murmured the quotation.

"Without subscribing to the view that 'to fight is but to die,' or indulging in any heroics about 'I have never turned my back upon don or devil yet,'" said John quietly, "I'm inclined to fight. We are safe until the morning, for if I know the police of Vigo, they will do nothing so uncomfortable as to attempt a midnight search of the harbour."

He went on to tell all he had seen, as he waited in the boat for the arrival of the missing Hollin.

"I was on the quay when the police appeared, and guessing something was up, I lay doggo in the boat. They have taken him to the central police station."

"What do you suggest?" asked Bobby. "We could hardly storm the citadel of the proud don."

John shook his head.

"It's a one-man job, and I'm willing to undertake it. I was thinking it out as I was rowing to the yacht. Orford, are there any fancy-dress costumes on board?"

" There are a whole heap. I had to pay two hundred and sixty dollars extra for the hire of them," said Mr. Orford. " But, boy, you're not going to take this job on alone; it has got to be organized——"

" I've organized it," said John shortly. "I spent years in this beastly place, unconsciously absorbing a great many organizable facts. The police are on duty all night, and the patrol men are not relieved until six in the morning. There are three people on duty at the station—an officer, a sergeant, and a man who acts as gaoler. I happen to know this, because one of my pupils—I used to give lessons here—was a policeman with an artistic bent, but there is very little about the force that I do not know."

Mr. Orford sighed.

" Go ahead," he said wearily. " Having got us into this trouble, I guess you'd better get us out again. You've spoilt my *chef d'œvre*, my young friend, and I can do nothing but sit right here and review a whole regiment of 'if's' parading by!"

When John had disappeared, a profound silence fell upon the group, a silence which Penelope broke.

"What has Hollin done?" she asked.

"What hasn't he done?" demanded Mr. Orford bitterly. "Say, Miss Pitt, there's nothing that boy hasn't done, from manslaughter to blowing a safe. And he has no more brains than a Paleolithic mastodon. It's sump'n terrible to think about!"

"But if he is so bad, why bother about him?" she asked, and knew she was being foolish, even if the dead silence which followed had not advertised her indiscretion. She was bewildered. Here was John taking a terrible risk for the sake of a man who was admittedly a criminal of the lowest mentality. It was on a par with the other mysteries of the *Polyantha*, the mystery of the flight down the Channel, the messages of wrecked aeroplanes, her drugging, and the amazing appearance of Cynthia Dorban.

     *   *   *   *   *

Inspector Spinner had a long but profitless interview with his charge in the cell in the Vigo police office. It was largely one-sided, for Hollin maintained a stolid silence, and only spoke to deny the truth of the inspector's surmise.

"My name's Jackson," he said for the twentieth time, "and I'll have the law on you for this. It's outrageous, that's what it is! Taking a poor sailorman and putting him in quod for something he never done!"

"You ought to be in heaven," said the weary inspector. "Anyway, I'll come along and see you in the morning, and then perhaps I'll be able to introduce you to a friend of yours."

"I got no friends," said Hollin. "I keep telling you, I don't know who you're talking about."

The steel grille clashed on him, and

7*

Hollin settled himself down on his hard pallet to sleep.

It was a quarter to three, and it was a pitch-black night, with the sky obscured with heavy banks of cloud. A thin rain was falling in the streets, and a chill wind induced the sensitive officer at the desk to reach down his cloak and wrap himself comfortably. His sergeant assistant, who had anticipated him in this act, sat nodding drowsily over his table, and only the solemn tick, tick of the clock, and the irregular beat of rain against the windows, disturbed the stillness.

A clock had just struck the hour, when there came a gentle knock at the closed door of the office. The sergeant did not hear it until he was aroused from his half-sleep by his superior.

"Open the door, man," said the officer sharply, and the sergeant, with a grunt, rose and, crossing the room, turned the key in the lock.

He opened the door.

"Who is that?" he asked sharply.

He could not see in the dark.

"It is I," said a deep, sepulchral voice.

The sergeant opened the door wide, and the dim figure that stood on the step outside stalked into the room, caught the edge of the door from the sergeant's hand, and slammed it.

The officer rose, open-mouthed, and stared at the visitor, as well he might.

The intruder, save for the black cloak about his shoulders, was dressed from head to foot in skin-tight scarlet. A black half-mask covered the upper part of his face, and a bedraggled cock's feather drooped drunkenly from his red skull-cap. But it was not so much the sinister apparition of a Mephistopheles in the middle of the night as the pistol he carried in his hand which made the policeman's jaw drop.

"Both of you will march to the cells," said the newcomer peremptorily, as he turned and locked the outer door of the office. "Let it be understood, *mio caballeros*, that I will shoot to kill if either of you raises his voice. Is that clear?"

"*Claro*," muttered the officer huskily. "This is a terrible thing you are doing, my friend——"

"Don't talk—walk!"

He ushered the pair into a long passage leading to the cells, and there he found the gaoler on duty. That rotund man was asleep.

"Take his keys; there is no need to wake him," said the intruder. "Now open the door where the American sailor is sleeping, and bring him out."

The officer struck an attitude, thrust his hands deep into his tunic, and raised his head, and stiffened.

"You may shoot, but I will not do this——" he began, and the red figure raised his pistol. Thereafter there was no difficulty.

Half-asleep and half-awake, Hollin came out into the passage, peering at the strange apparition.

John only waited long enough to snip the telephone wires before he dragged the dazed prisoner into the street, locked the door and flung the key into the roadway.

"Now, Hollin, run," he said.

"Oh, it's you, is it?" gasped Hollin, who was not used to violent exercise. "Why didn't you bring a cab?"

"What's the matter with the road?" hissed the other in his ear. "Save your breath, you windy devil."

They passed one policeman, who was huddled up in a doorway sheltered from the rain, which was now pelting down, and he did no more than give them a sleepy "*Buenos noches*" as they passed at a walk, for John had sighted the glowing end of the policeman's cigar.

Day was breaking when Mr. Hollin came wearily to the deck of the *Polyantha*, and no sooner had his feet touched the deck, when he heard the clang of the telegraph and the thud of the screws. The yacht was already under way, heading for the entrance of Vigo Harbour.

"Now, you brute," said John, an awe-inspiring figure despite his soddened scarlet, "change your clothes—quick! You are going a little journey with me."

"What do you mean?" demanded the other truculently.

"I mean the *Polyantha* will be searched directly she comes back from this little trip to the high seas, and I'm taking pretty good care that you are not on board her."

Hollin was glad to get back to his cabin, for there was security. He had carefully cached the two formidable guns that he had commandeered on his arrival on the yacht, and these he discovered where he had left them, and returned to the saloon to find that John had made a quick change, and was waiting for him, and with him, in addition to Penelope Pitt, were two strangers, a man and a woman.

The woman was talking volubly.

" It is disgraceful, monstrous! I will not leave the ship," she said shrilly.

" You will do as you are told," replied John, and there was a hardness in his voice which Penelope Pitt had never heard before.

" The discomfort, if any, will not endure for longer than a day. On the contrary, my discomfort, if the police come on board the *Polyantha* and find us here, will last considerably longer than a day. Mrs. Dorban " —his grave eyes were fixed on hers—" I more than suspect that you people are responsible for the tragedy of my life. I do not quite understand how the plot was worked, but proof will come, and it will be a day of reckoning for you. Your motive at least I know. Whether or not you were in this scheme which brought me to the very edge of hell has yet to be discovered. You can understand this much—that I shall stop at nothing, and that I shall deal with you ruthlessly if there is need."

He stopped short at the sentence, and looked at the woman, and from the woman into the brown eyes of Arthur Dorban, and then his gaze wandered to Hollin.

"Before the *Polyantha* clears the mouth of the harbour she will stop, and we are rowing ashore—these two people, Miss Pitt and I, and you, Hollin. There is a secluded cave, inaccessible except from the sea—I know the place because I used to play there when I was a child," he added shortly. "We shall stay there for twenty-four hours, it may be longer. The *Polyantha* will pick us up in good time. The yacht is certain to be intercepted along the coast and searched, and it is very necessary that none of us should be found on board. You understand that, Hollin?" His eyes dropped to the guns at the man's hips and he smiled faintly. Then, with a beckoning nod to the girl, he went up on deck and she followed. "I am

very sorry that you are to have this incon-
venience, Miss Pitt," he said; "and after
our unpardonable treatment of you, it isn't
fair that you should be further troubled.
This particular experience will not be as unpleasant as it appears to our friends in the
chilly hours of the morning. The cave is
weatherproof, it is a delightful little spot,
and we are taking a plentiful supply of
provisions."

"I don't mind a bit," she said. "John—
I suppose I ought to call you John, although
I am sure that is not your name—won't you
please take me a little into your confidence,
and tell me what is the meaning of this
mystery?"

He hesitated for a moment, and then:

"I trust you completely; some day I will
tell you."

There was no particular reason why the
consciousness of his trust should send the
colour to her face and give her a sense of
complete achievement. She was puzzled;

and for the first time in her life was something of an enigma to herself. That feeling of having accomplished something had its reaction in an annoyance. Why was she so placed that she had made him trust her?

She was almost cheerful as, wrapped in a heavy coat, and that protected by an oil-skin, she went down the little companion-way and stepped into the bobbing motor-boat.

Cynthia and Arthur Dorban were already there, huddled miserably in the for'ard well. Hollin, his armaments conspicuously displayed, had taken the most comfortable seat aft, but was sharply ordered forward to make room for the girl.

"All right?" boomed Orford's voice from the deck.

"All right, sir," said John cheerfully, and a minute later the little motor-boat, dangerously overloaded, as John knew, was pitching and tossing toward the shore.

John ran the nose of the boat on to the gently shelving beach, and the passengers landed as best they could—all except Penelope; John waded into the sea and carried her ashore.

" That's all, Simpson," he said to the man in charge of the boat. "Go back to the yacht."

" Good luck, sir !" said the sailor.

Iᴛ was still very dark, but John led the way unerringly, walking straight toward the cliffs. Suddenly he flashed the light of an electric torch before him, and Penelope saw a narrow and dark fissure in the face of the rock.

"Here is our robber's cave," said John. "I think we had better get in, because the tide is coming up and the water usually floods the floor. Farther back you will find a sort of natural platform where we shall be dry and cosy."

He put down the big basket he had carried from the boat, opened it, and took out a lantern and applied a light to the wick. The cave was deep and narrow, and, glancing back, Penelope saw that the entrance was so shaped that the light could not be visible from the open sea.

She guessed the roof of the cave was nearly a hundred feet above them. At the back of it was a rock platform of which John had spoken, and up this he leapt, stretching out his hand to help the girl.

From this platform were three separate openings, placed so symmetrically that it seemed almost as though they were the work of man.

"They lead to nowhere in particular, but if we have to spend the night that on the left," he pointed, "if my memory serves me aright, will make an admirable sleeping-place for Mrs. Dorban and her husband. You can sleep in there, Miss Pitt. There is half a mile of cave for you to wander in, and I'll give you each a lantern, and that will be necessary even after the sun gets up."

Penelope had not spoken a word to Cynthia, and she imagined that the woman would not desire to speak to her. She was amazed and indignant, therefore, when, with her most gracious smile, Cynthia said:

"How on earth did you get on to this wretched yacht, Penelope?"

John saved the girl the trouble of replying.

"You will have no communication whatever with Miss Pitt," he said sternly. "Whatever is the outcome of this business, I am determined that you shall stand your trial for the vilest act of your life, Mrs. Dorban."

"I would like to remind you that you are speaking to my wife," Arthur Dorban broke his long silence. "And as to Miss Pitt, she has behaved abominably. She has made the most reckless charges against my honour——"

John laughed.

"Slico," he said, "you are amusing. Your honour! A cheap card-sharper, the associate of every thief in Europe—your honour!"

Mr. Dorban did not seem greatly perturbed.

"Whatever I am or have been is beside

the question," he said. "I know what you are, my friend!"

Penelope stared at the man; there was a threat in the tone which she could not understand. The mystery of the *Polyantha* was gradually narrowing to the mystery of John the sailor.

"Of one thing you may be certain," said John quietly. "That if I knew you as definitely as you know me, there would be a very unpleasant time ahead for Mr. Arthur Dorban. And now, if you will be kind enough not to talk, I shall be obliged."

He took from the basket a small oblong box, searched for, and found, a fishing-rod, from which a long wire dangled, and disappeared through the mouth of the cave. After a quarter of an hour he came back, carrying the box and the fishing-rod. These he deposited on the platform.

"They are smarter than I gave them credit for," he said. "Their wireless is working overtime. I couldn't quite understand all they were talking about, but I guessed that Vigo is in communication with a warship which is somewhere cruising along the coast, so *Polyantha* will have early morning visitors. Hollin, you are a lucky man."

Hollin, sitting glumly on the edge of the platform, smoking a short wooden pipe, grunted.

"How do you know all this?" he asked. "What is that?"

He frowned down at the litle box.

"It is a portable wireless," said John, "with which Mr. Orford thoughtfully provided me. If they had been using the Morse code they would have baffled me, but happily they are telephoning. They know you, and all about you, by the way, Hollin."

Mr. Hollin shifted uncomfortably.

The cave was gradually becoming lighter. The reflected light through the doorway enabled them to dispense with their lanterns, and with the light came the sea. It came foaming whitely, first to the entrance of the cave, and then along the sandy bed, and finally covered the floor, rising until there was only a foot's space of the cave entrance uncovered.

John watched the diminishing glimpse of daylight with an anxious eye. At certain seasons of the year the entrance was wholly covered, and the water reached the platform. There was no danger from this, for the height of the cave gave them a plentiful supply of oxygen, providing they were not cut off too long a time from the life-giving air outside. Presently, however, the water began to subside, and he heaved a sigh of relief and set about preparing their breakfast.

Dorban and his wife had withdrawn to the entrance of their "private cave," and were conferring together in low voices. Hollin sat crouched up against the wall of the cave, his legs drawn up underneath him in tailor-fashion, dozing, and Penelope and her strange *vis-à-vis* were left alone.

Presently she broached the subject which was in her mind.

"These people seem to know all about you; is it—is it something to your discredit?"

He nodded.

"Yes and no," he answered. "They know nothing which touches my honour; much that affects my safety."

And with this cryptic reply she had to be satisfied.

Cynthia's eye had not left the two. She saw John stooping toward the girl, guessed from his lowered voice that he was speaking confidentially, and whispered to her husband.

"You are mad," said Arthur Dorban calmly, when she had whispered her suspicion. "What difference does it make, suppose he does fall in love with her?"

"Suppose he marries her?" said Cynthia.

Arthur Dorban frowned.

"Marry her?" he repeated.

"Suppose he marries her; suppose there is a child of the marriage, you fool," said the woman angrily.

"How could they marry? It is you who are a fool," said Arthur. "By this time every Spanish port will be watched for the *Polyantha*, and every other port in the world."

"The captain could marry them," she interrupted him. "Every sea captain is entitled to perform the marriage ceremony on the high seas. Don't you know that? You've travelled on ships, I believe," she said sarcastically.

"I have never travelled with the captain," said the urbane Mr. Dorban. "I think you are exaggerating the possibilities, Cynthia. She's pretty, isn't she?"

He asked this quite dispassionately, and as dispassionately Mrs. Dorban regarded the profile of the unconscious girl.

"Yes, I suppose she is," she said. "Have you spoken to the man?"

"He's asleep," said Arthur Dorban, glancing at the slumbering Hollin.

"When our gaoler leaves the cave, wake this fellow, Arthur."

A little while later John waded out to make a reconnaissance. He was wearing seaman's thigh-boots, and was the only member of the party so equipped.

"There is nothing in sight, you people. I think we'll have breakfast. I see you have aroused my friend Mr. Hollin."

Dorban had done no more than waken the ex-convict, for the time at his disposal had been too short. He had an opportunity later, when the waters had departed, and John had taken the girl to the beach for an airing.

"If she can go out, we can go out," grumbled Hollin. "If he thinks I am going to stay in this hole all day, he's made a mistake."

Mr. Dorban nodded encouragingly.

"He treats you like a dog," he said. "I can understand his behaving to us that way, because we are not friends of his, but a man who has helped him as you have——"

"That's a fact. They treat me like dirt," said Mr. Hollin indignantly, "and just because I said a few words about that young dame." He jerked his head to the entrance of the cave. "This John up and told me that he'd beat the head off me. That's a nice way to treat a friend!"

"Why do you serve him?" asked Cynthia softly. "I dare say he has promised you a lot of money, but how do you know that he will keep his promise?"

Mr. Hollin shifted uncomfortably.

"He wouldn't dare——" he began.

"Are you sure?" Cynthia's eyebrows rose perceptibly. "What is to prevent their settling with you before the yacht reaches South America? It will be quite easy some dark night, you know, Mr. Hollin—— I don't wish to alarm you, but I feel it is my duty to tell you what kind of people you are dealing with. What is to prevent their shooting you and throwing you overboard? You think that John would hesitate—a man with his record?"

Mr. Hollin had not the slightest idea of what the record was; but he did know that John had uttered a significant threat one evening, and he began to question his wisdom of trusting to the word of his host.

"They are returning now," said Cynthia in a low voice. "When we get back to the *Polyantha* I want a little talk with you."

Hollin nodded.

Coming from the bright light outside into the gloom of the cave, John did not for the moment observe that the Dorbans had altered their position and were with his charge.

In the afternoon John took the girl aside.

"I am going to one of these caves to sleep," he said. "I must be wide awake to-night. I want you to sit at the entrance and call me if anything happens. Can you use a pistol?"

"I've fired several," she smiled, "but I am afraid I am not an accurate shot."

"Don't look at me," he said in a conversational tone. "I am slipping a little Browning into the pocket of your oilskin. There—do you feel?"

"It is very heavy," she said. "What am I to do with it?"

"Shoot," he said laconically, "if the necessity arises. I do not imagine that the Dorbans will play any tricks, but I do not trust them. If any of them attempt to leave the cave, call me."

John had been asleep for an hour when Mr. Hollin stretched himself, and, with his hands in his pockets, strolled toward the entrance of the cave.

"You are not to go out, Hollin," she commanded.

He looked round.

"I don't take orders from women," he said contemptuously; and then, seeing her turn to the inner cave, he said hastily: "Oh, well, if you are going to make a fuss, I won't go."

At five o'clock she made tea from the spirit-stove, and carried in a cup to the slumbering John. She had fallen naturally into the position of his lieutenant, and sensed with some amusement the antagonism of her fellow-prisoners.

At seven o'clock the tide began to come in again, and it was well after ten when John waded out to the open.

" No sign of *Polyantha*," he said, as he returned. " I hardly expect her before midnight. In fact, it will be difficult to get aboard at high tide."

All night long he alternately watched and listened, his receiver clamped to his ears, the girl steadying the frail pole which carried his aerial. Nearing dawn, he picked up a voice from the ether.

" Not to-night, John."

It was repeated at ten-minute intervals, and he thought he recognized Bobby's voice.

"That's that," said John with a sigh. "We're locked in for another day. Now, young woman, you must sleep. There is no chance of getting away. And your little cave isn't really a bad one. Come along."

They passed into the cave together, and had mounted the rocky platform when he hissed a warning. The sound of rowlocks had reached his ears, and presently she heard it too—the steady clump-clump of oars.

"Is it——?" she whispered.

"No. They would have sent the motorboat for us. Wait!"

He came softly to the floor of the cave and disappeared into the gloom. Then she saw him dimly in the reflected light of the dawn. She followed, and he seemed to expect her, for he slipped a little further along the cave wall to make room for her. There came a voice.

"This is where they'll be. He was in the habit of coming to a cave somewhere around here when he was a child."

8

John's lips moved at her ear.

"Spinner. An English detective," but she was incapable of response.

And then another voice spoke.

"If *he* is here, my friend is here, Inspector. My two friends, Mr. and Mrs. Arthur Dorban."

She felt the man stiffen and he made a movement toward the mouth of the cave. Instinctively she pulled him back.

"Where are you going?" she demanded in a terrified whisper.

"I'm going to the owner of that voice," said John between his teeth.

But she held him back with all her strength.

"You're mad!" she said desperately. "Besides—I know him; his name is Whiplow!"

SPINNER was speaking in Spanish, and he was evidently addressing some person in authority. John guessed that it was the captain of police whose calm he had invaded.

"Is there a cave here, Señor Captain?"

"No; there is a large cave on the other side of the bluff. I do not remember any cave on this beach, and I have been in Vigo since I was a boy, señor."

"What does he say?" asked Whiplow's voice impatiently.

"He says that the cave——"

The remainder of the detective's words were drowned by the sound of oars as the boatmen resumed their rowing. It came fainter and fainter.

"Whiplow—that is the man! Bobby always thought it was he, but could never be sure."

He was talking to himself, and she could not hear all he was saying. Then he spoke directly to her.

"You are sure that was Whiplow?" he asked in a low voice.

"Quite sure. I should know his voice anywhere," she replied.

There was an interregnum of silence, and then John said—and again it seemed that he was speaking his thoughts aloud :

"The question is, Will they come back after they have searched the other cave? There is another, you know—a much bigger one than this."

They waited for nearly an hour, listening, and presently they heard the oars again, but this time the boat passed the entrance to the cave and went on toward Vigo.

It was now growing light, and Pen was feeling inexpressibly tired. Though he could not see her, he must have sensed her weariness, for in a brisker tone than usual he ordered her off to bed.

"Won't you tell me," she almost pleaded, "what it is all about? I feel so confused and bewildered, and—a little frightened."

"There is nothing for you to fear," he said, almost gruffly. "And as for telling you"—he laughed softly to himself—"well, I was afraid you'd have to know this evening. At any rate, you'll know very soon."

He put on his pocket-lamp to show her the way into the cave, and in the circle of its light he saw a figure standing on the edge of the platform. It was Mrs. Dorban.

"Is anything wrong?" she asked sharply.

"Everything is remarkably right," said John cheerfully.

"I thought I heard you speaking to somebody outside," she said.

John did not answer until he had helped the girl to the platform, and then:

"Yes, it was a friend of yours," he said, "but he wasn't speaking to me."

"A friend of mine?" she answered quickly. "Whom do you mean?"

Again he tantalized her by his silence, and she asked the question again.

"Whiplow," he said.

He had lit a candle, and by its light he saw her expression change.

"Whiplow?" she repeated incredulously. "You are lying! How could he be here—besides, who is Mr. Whiplow?"

John smiled.

"I thought perhaps you might not know him," he said ironically. "But nevertheless, he was here—Miss Pitt recognized his voice."

The woman recovered her self-possession in a moment.

"How ridiculous you are!" she said. "I know Mr. Whiplow. He called upon my husband once when I was in London. But to say that he is a friend of mine is absurd. Did you speak to him?"

She was eyeing John shrewdly.

"I did not," said John. "The mere fact that I am here is a proof that we had no exchange of confidences. Some day, however, I shall speak to him, and I have an idea that it will be a very bad day for you, Mrs. Dorban."

The woman's self-possession was extra-ordinary. She could even, in that moment of crisis, smile.

"How romantic you are!" she sneered. "That almost sounds like an extract from a popular melodrama!"

With a shrug of her shoulders she turned and walked back to the cave where Arthur Dorban was sleeping. She found her way to him in the dark and shook him gently, and Slico was instantly awake.

"What is it?" he asked in a low voice.

"Whiplow is here," she answered in the same tone.

"Here? In the cave?"

"No, you fool. But he's in Vigo, and apparently he was searching for us. Probably he was in a boat, and our friend John saw him."

Arthur Dorban was very wide awake now.

"Whiplow here!" he mused. "The swine! He swore he was leaving for the United States by the next boat."

"For a man with your past you are a very simple person," she said patiently. "Whiplow has been shadowing us, and must have followed us through France and Spain. And when you come to think of it, Arthur, it wasn't likely that he would leave the nest of the golden eggs so readily."

"Did—John see him?" asked Dorban quickly.

She shook her head.

"No. That infernal girl recognized his voice."

"Then you think—John knows?"

"He's been guessing for a long time, I suspect," she said coolly. "So long as he didn't recognize the voice also, there is nothing very much to fear. Arthur, we must lose no further time. Have you spoken to Hollin?"

"I had a talk with him," said Arthur Dorban. There was a scratch and a splutter of flame as he lit a cigarette. "I think he will be easy," he went on, "if he is worked right. We can do nothing here."

She made a movement of impatience.

"Where else?" she demanded savagely. "This is the only place where we can act. You are both armed——"

"Unfortunately we are not," interrupted her husband. "During Hollin's absence from the ship somebody got at his guns, extracted the cartridges and substituted dummies. He only found that out to-night; and under the circumstances I thought it was wise to examine my own automatic. Exactly the same change had been made. The magazine is empty, the cartridge in the breech is a spent one. My dear Cynthia, we are dealing with some very clever people, and it was stupid in us to think that we should catch them so easily. When I hid my gun I ought to have known that at the very first opportunity a careful search would

8*

be made of the cabin. That search was made during the few minutes we were brought to the saloon, the live cartridges were taken out and the others substituted. It was the same with Hollin."

"Why didn't they take the weapons away altogether?" she asked, but recognized the futility of that question before he attempted to answer.

Day came—a long and a dreary wait, relieved only by the flooding of the cave when the tide rose. At ten o'clock that night John, standing on the beach before the cave, heard the soft chug-chug of a motor-boat, and presently heard the grind of it as the bow was beached.

He went forward cautiously, and Bobby's voice hailed him.

"All well, John?"

"Everything's all right, Bobby."

"Get on board quick; we've a long journey. The *Polyantha's* standing ten miles out, but luckily the sea is smooth."

John went into the cave and called his party together. In preparation for departure the basket had been packed, and in a few minutes the crowded little boat was labouring toward the open sea.

It was nearly midnight before they came alongside, and Cynthia, who had had a prosaic attack of sea-sickness, was glad to get on board. Nor was Penelope sorry to lie down on her comfortable bed.

She did not see John that night; she was far too tired to seek him out, and she fell asleep long before the *Polyantha's* propellers began to revolve. Once in the night she was wakened by the roar of the siren, and got up to look through the porthole. The ship was running through a thick bank of fog, and her speed had been considerably reduced.

When she finally awoke, the cabin was flooded with diffused sunlight, and the clock by the side of her bed marked half-past ten. Inside the cabin door was a tray. The coffee was quite cold, and the toast dry and un-appetizing. She got into her dressing-gown and rang the bell, and presently came a tap at the door and John's voice wished her "Good-morning!"

" I GUESSED you were asleep," he said, " and I've brought you some more coffee. Will you please remember that you're supposed to lock your cabin door at night?"

" I was so tired," she excused herself, as she took the tray round the edge of the door. "Where are we?"

"We are somewhere," vaguely. " I was never a whale at mathematics, and navigation is a mystery unsolved. I think we're going south-westwards; as near as I can judge, we are heading for the Canary Islands. Hurry up and dress; Mr. Orford wants to see you."

There was something in his tone which she could not quite understand—an awkwardness, a discomfort, which were wholly foreign to him. His reference to Mr. Orford was hurried and almost incoherent, and he vanished almost before he had finished the sentence.

She found Mr. Orford sitting in his favourite deck-chair under a little awning which had been evidently spread for him; and Mr. Orford was not looking very happy. There seemed to be more creases in his face; his eyes appeared to have retreated still further behind the fleshy slits which marked their position; and his big hands, usually folded so complacently across his expansive waistcoat, were restless and busy, now fiddling with the arm of the chair, now twiddling the buttons of his coat.

"Good-morning, Miss Pitt! Sit you down here."

She obeyed, wondering.

"Miss Pitt," he began, after clearing his throat, and she was amazed to find that he, too, showed signs of nervousness, "in all organizations the human factor stands for ten per cent. of error. Some sanguine and ignorant people put a plus mark against the human factor, but with me it's minus all the time. Machinery's true and honest and works to the second and the fraction of a second. You can organize fuel to the foot pound. You can even calculate upon the elements to within five per cent. of error. But when the human factor comes in, you've got to make a large margin of allowance, or organization goes to hell—if you will forgive the language."

She shook her head, not knowing what to say, for he was quite incomprehensible.

" I can organize a journey from London to Constantinople, Bagdad, Jaffa, Cincinnati, Sao Paulo—any old place—and can be sure the schedule will work to the hour. But when I organize a journey from London to Gibraltar, and the man that's taking that journey stops off at Cordova to have a look round the cathedral, and meets a pretty girl and takes her to lunch and misses the cars —why, then, my schedule goes——" He snapped his finger. "And why? Because the human element, the desire for a good lunch and a penchant for a pretty face, has sidetracked my client beyond hope of salvation. The human factor is my nightmare; it is the one factor that keeps Xenocrates Orford in a perpetual fret of worry and despair. You have seen a remarkable example of how the human factor, in its deadliest aspect, has made my organization look like a ball of string after the cat has had it." He bit off the end of a cigar savagely and lit it before he went on. " Now, Miss Pitt " —he half-slewed round to face her—" you've helped to make my prospects as cheerful as a wet Sunday in the city of Glasgow."

" I ?" she said guiltily.

" You," he nodded. " We should not have gone to Vigo if you hadn't wanted clothes. And you wouldn't have wanted clothes if you hadn't been here. You've turned every darned switch on my track."

" I'm very sorry, Mr. Orford," she said.

"I can't help feeling that what you say is right. I do not know what the organization is, and why we are wandering over the Atlantic I cannot even guess. I realize it's for some very important and vital reason, and I do feel that in some way—though it has not been exactly my fault—I have been responsible for your change of plan. If I can do anything——"

"You can," he said, staring steadfastly at the sea. "You can marry John."

She half-rose from her chair, but his big hand dropped on her shoulder.

"Wait," he said. "I'm a family man by nature, though I've never been married. I'm chock-full of the milk of human kindness, and I wouldn't hurt you or any other woman, not willingly and knowingly. But you can put things right, and suffer no injury yourself, if you will carry out my suggestion."

"But marry John? That is impossible," she said incoherently. "I hardly know him. Of course, I realize he's not a deck hand, but that he's somebody very important in your scheme. And I like him very much. But marriage!"

"Lots of people don't even like the people they're going to marry," said the philosophical Mr. Orford, not taking his eyes from the horizon. "And this marriage will be —well, it won't be the ordinary sort of marriage. I can't say that you'll part at the church door, because there'll be no church. And anyway, you couldn't part from your husband unless we set him adrift in a small boat. But that's all beside the point. I tell you, you can render me and him the greatest service that one man can render to another, if you'll agree to marry him. The captain has the authority, and you can confirm the marriage in a real church afterwards—if you have the opportunity."

"But I don't want to marry," she protested.

"Maybe you're engaged?" suggested Mr. Orford.

"Of course I'm not engaged," she said scornfully. "It isn't necessary that I should be engaged to object to—oh, it's too absurd!"

Mr. Orford pulled at his cigar.

"The human factor," he said softly, speaking to himself. "You can't get over that." He sat smoking furiously a little while. "I will give you a hundred thousand dollars if you will marry John," he said in a matter-of-fact tone.

She shook her head.

"I would give you an income that you've never dreamt of——"

"It is no use, Mr. Orford," she said quietly. "Money has no influence in this matter. Does John know you are asking me this?"

He nodded.

"John is kind o' shy, I guess," he said; "and, anyway, he doesn't expect you to agree."

"He, at any rate, has a little intelligence," she said with some asperity as she rose.

He looked up at her.

"Miss Pitt, will you marry John to save his life?" he asked quietly.

"That is a supposition——"

"It's no supposition, believe me," said the stout man grimly. "I'm using an argument I promised him I would not use. If certain things happen in the next month, and he at that time is unmarried"—he took the cigar from his teeth and examined it thoughtfully —"why, I wouldn't risk ten cents for his life."

She could only stare at him.

"Do you seriously mean that?"

"I was never more serious," said Mr. Orford. He got up and waddled to the side and glared down at the sea. "You may not be able to save him from imprisonment," he went on in the same even tone. "Somehow, I don't think you can do that, though I had hopes until you came along. But you might save his life. They've tried twice to kill him, you know," he said suddenly, looking at her.

"Who?"

Mr. Orford jerked his head to the companion-way.

"The Dorbans?" she gasped.

"Twice," he nodded. "And they will succeed eventually."

"I don't know what it all means," said Pen in despair. "It sounds so dreadful that I can hardly believe——"

"You know Mrs. Dorban, and you can believe a great deal about her," said Mr. Orford.

She shivered.

"Well, I'm not going to worry you any more, Miss Pitt. We'll have to get along as well as we can." He threw his cigar into the sea, and watched it with an interest which would have been comical in any other circumstances as it disappeared into the white wake of the ship. "I've got to the point where even the failure of my organization doesn't rattle me any. The engineer has become the spectator, and I guess I'm getting a little fatalistic."

He rested his elbows on the rail, and his face was a picture of gloom, and still she stood, hesitating, her mind in a whirl, her heart beating at a tremendous rate.

"Suppose I agreed, Mr. Orford," she said a little huskily, "what would it mean to me?"

"I am not going to urge you," he said.

"But what would it mean?"

"To you it would mean no more than a change of name, Miss Pitt," said he, facing her. "You would be as free then as you are now—more free, I think, because you would have money. I know that isn't any consideration," he went on quickly; "but never despise money, Miss Pitt. It is everything that is material, and the material is very essential in this materialistic existence. And it gives you a whole heap of leisure to cultivate your spiritual side," he added with such a beaming smile that she laughed.

"I'll think it over." She frowned. "No, I won't think it over, I'll tell you now. If in all seriousness you tell me that this—marriage—may be the means of saving his life, I will agree. Who will marry us?"

"The captain," said Mr. Orford, very alert. "And it can be fixed——"

He stopped suddenly and raised his hand in warning. Then, bending over the side of the yacht, looked down, and with his finger to his lips he led her away from the rail.

"I wonder whether they could hear," he said.

"They?—the Dorbans?"

He nodded.

"We were carrying on our interesting conversation immediately above their open porthole," said he. "I guess I'm getting old."

CYNTHIA DORBAN, kneeling bolt upright on the settee, with her ear turned to the sea, had heard almost every word. Mr. Arthur Dorban, lying on his bed, a book on his upbent knees, a cigarette between his lips, watched the tense figure of his wife without knowing the character of the conversation she was overhearing.

"Well?" he asked, as she slipped down to the floor of the cabin.

"She is going to marry him," said Cynthia Dorban between her teeth. "I told you what Orford would do."

Mr. Dorban carefully extinguished his cigarette and got up to his feet.

"When is this to happen?" he asked quietly.

"To-day—to-morrow—how do I know?" she snapped.

Mr. Arthur Dorban put on his jacket very deliberately, opened the door of the cabin and looked down the narrow alley-way. The next cabin was in the occupation of the doctor; the cabin beyond was Bobby's; on the other side of the alley-way Mr. Orford was housed; further on, the chief engineer had his quarters. The captain's cabin was exactly opposite theirs, but usually he slept in the chart-house immediately behind the navigation bridge.

Arthur Dorban tried the door, and it was, as usual, locked.

"Go for'ard to the foot of the companion-ladder and keep watch," he said.

"What are you going to do?" she asked. "You know we're not allowed on deck."

"Don't jabber; do as you're told," he snarled, and she went along the alley-way without further question.

Returning to the cabin, he took from his suitcase a bunch of keys and tried them, one after another upon the captain's door. The time at his disposal was short, and any moment one of the deck hands might come along and detect him, and there was no time to waste.

A naturally indolent man, he had hoped that by his cunning he might obviate the necessity for adopting this drastic method, or, at best, that it would be deferred for some time. But now he recognized the serious consequences which were involved in Penelope's agreement.

None of the keys fitted. Hanging on the wall of the alley-way was a glass case with an emergency axe to be used in case of fire, and the case was not locked. He took out the axe and, stepping back, brought it down with a crash upon the door, then, wedging the edge between the door and the frame, he wrenched it open.

A quick glance round—there was nobody in sight—and it was hardly likely that the noise he had made would be heard upon the deck above the drumming of the turbines.

The cabin was a large one, furnished with a desk, a brass bedstead, and a tall wardrobe. He pulled open the drawers of the desk. In the first of these he found what he was seeking—a pair of automatic pistols and two large boxes of cartridges. There would be an arms chest too, he thought, as he tore open the package and loaded one of the pistols. This he found under the bed—a flat wooden box painted black and unlocked. Within were half a dozen heavy Army revolvers, two rifles, fifty packages of ammunition, and half a dozen pairs of handcuffs. These he transferred in two journeys to his own cabin. His wife was watching from the far end of the alley-way, and he beckoned her.

"Find Hollin."

She had seen Hollin at the head of the companion-stairs, cleaning the brasswork; for since he had returned to the ship Mr. Hollin's position had undergone a radical change for the worse. She flew back along the alley-way and called the man down, and at that moment the captain appeared in the doorway leading from the deck.

"Where are you going?" he demanded.

"Run!" hissed Cynthia, and Hollin obeyed.

Old as he was, the captain was agile, and he came racing along the alley-way after the man, but stopped dead before the levelled pistol in Arthur Dorban's hand.

"If you shout I'll kill you," said Dorban. "Go in there." He pointed to the captain's cabin.

"What have you been doing?" demanded the old man wrathfully.

Leading from the cabin was a small bathroom, and into this Captain Willit was thrust and the door locked on him.

"What's the game?"

Hollin's slow mind hardly grasped the changed position.

"Take this," said Dorban. He thrust a Webley into the man's hand. "Cynthia, you stay here and watch the captain. See that the old man doesn't get away."

He raced up the companion-way on to the deck, Hollin, a little dumbfounded, a little uneasy, behind him. Mr. Orford was talking to the girl when Arthur Dorban appeared, and he was not long in realizing just what had happened.

" Say——" he began.

" You make a noise and you're a dead man," said Dorban. "Watch those two, Hollin, while I settle with the people on the bridge."

Only one of the deck hands and the quartermaster on duty were visible as he ran along the boat-deck. Dorban knew that the men were negligible quantities, and that the only weapons on board the ship were those which were safely locked in his cabin—unless, perhaps, Bobby or John were armed. Luck was with him, for he found these two men on the bridge talking with the second officer.

" Hands up ! "

John spun round to meet the threat of his enemy's weapon.

" It isn't necessary for me to tell you," said Arthur Dorban in his quiet, even tone, " that I shall be perfectly justified in the eyes of the law if I shoot every one of you. Turn about, you two men ! "

John obeyed. He guessed what had happened, and he knew that any resistance at this moment was likely to lead to serious trouble. A handcuff was snapped about his wrists, and a second later Bobby was also manacled.

" Now, gentlemen," said Dorban, addressing the startled chief officer and the quartermaster at the wheel, " you probably realize that you're in a very serious position. I have taken upon myself to arrest the captain. You may escape the consequence of your illegal act if you carry out my instructions."

The chief officer was a tall, gaunt man, with an expression which years of disappointment had permanently soured.

"What are your instructions, might I ask?" he demanded.

"That you navigate the ship back to England."

"You can navigate her yourself," said the chief officer. "This is an act of piracy, and if there's any trouble coming it is yours."

He gripped the hand of the telegraph and rang the engines to stop, and then, pushing past the annoyed Mr. Dorban, he walked aft. The quartermaster, however, was a man of another type, and when Dorban had got his prisoners below and locked into a cabin, he returned to interview this sailor, with satisfactory results. Coming down, he found his wife on deck, and with her was Hollin, who had found his way almost instinctively to the whisky decanter, and was at that moment taking a large and generous view of life.

"I have persuaded the quartermaster to take us into Cadiz," he said. "The engineers have agreed to remain on duty, so we shall get through."

"What about the girl?"

He shrugged his shoulders.

"She is in her cabin," he said, and tried to change the subject; but here she was immediately interested.

"Are you going to take the girl into Cadiz, too? The girl who saw the notes and the pictures? The girl I tried to drown?"

"Who is to believe her?" he asked, with an appearance of testiness, though she was well enough acquainted with him to know that he was half-uneasy in his mind. "She has no evidence to support any statement she can make; and the mere fact that she's with this man is enough to condemn her."

She appeared to be satisfied with his view, though Arthur Dorban was not deceived.

"I can't afford to worry about these side issues," he said. "I've quite enough anxiety as it is. Hollin, you go forward and watch the men's quarters. I will stay on the bridge to make certain the quartermaster doesn't play me false. We ought to fall in with a warship in a few hours. The quartermaster told me that they are as thick as flies in these waters—Gibraltar is only about three hundred miles away. You go below, Cynthia, and keep an eye upon the prisoners."

In Bobby's cabin the two young men sat down to consider the situation. They sat down together because there was no help for it, since they were handcuffed one to the other.

"I think we can say that this is the end of the adventure," said John with unnatural calmness. "I'm hating myself, Bobby, for having brought you into this scrape."

"I'm hating myself worse for not having got you out of it," said Bobby bitterly. "I was mad not to realize how simple it was to put ourselves in the hands of these people."

John was whistling softly, his eyes fixed upon the carpet.

"I wonder what they have done with Miss Pitt?" he asked suddenly.

"She's in her cabin; I do know that," said

Bobby. " I heard him telling Hollin as they went past the door just now. What do you think they'll do?"

John shook his head.

" They'll probably make for the nearest port and hand us over," he said. " If the jolly old Xenocrates organizes us out of this mess, I'm going to put up a silver statue to him."

" Make it gold," said Bobby drearily. " One dream is as inexpensive as the other. Where is Orford, by the way?"

" In the doctor's cabin, next door," replied John. He got up and knocked at the wall. There came an answering tap. " Yes, he's there. Poor old Xenocrates!"

He looked down at the steel band about his wrist, and for the thirtieth time tried to slip his hand through.

" It's no use," he groaned; " and to think that only two people are holding the ship!"

" I suppose Hollin is of some use," said Bobby dubiously.

"I wasn't thinking of Hollin. I was thinking of Cynthia Dorban. She is the real commander-in-chief of that confederation." He stopped, and Bobby saw his eyes brighten. "I wonder!" he said softly, and without explaining the subject of his wonder, he kicked heavily at the door of the cabin. Presently Cynthia Dorban's voice cried sharply:

"What do you want?"

"Are you going to let us have any food, or do you intend starving us to death?" asked John.

"If you want food you'll have to get it yourselves," replied Cynthia. The lock snapped and the door opened, revealing Cynthia, automatic in hand. "You can go along to the pantry and get enough food to last you for two days," she said. "At the end of that time you will be fed by the Spanish authorities."

Now Bobby was not hungry, and the very

thought of food revolted him. He could only marvel that his companion at such a moment could confess to an appetite.

"If you try any of your tricks," said Cynthia, as she followed him along the alley-way——

"You'll shoot—I know all about that," said John, "and I quite believe you. If it were the chicken-hearted Slico, I should not be so easily convinced."

The pantry was a small storehouse behind the ship's galley, which, when they entered it, was deserted.

"Hurry up and get what you want," said Cynthia, standing on guard at the doorway of the kitchen.

John led his companion into the small, dark room where the food was stored. He made no attempt to open the ice-chest; instead, he put up his hand to the wall, felt for a small knob and moved it cautiously. It was too dark to see, but he counted the tiny nodes and presently he let the indicator rest on the sixth, pressed a push-button and took down a small receiver.

"Sing, Bobby," he hissed. "Sing, I tell you," and Bobby's voice rose unmusically.

"Is that you, Penelope?" asked John urgently. He had remembered that there was a telephonic communication between the pantry and each of the big cabins.

"Yes, where are you?"

"Never mind that," said John. "You know Bobby's cabin? It is immediately under the red ventilator. Can you get hold of any kind of firearm and drop it over the side at the end of a piece of string, so that we can reach it?"

"I'm not allowed out of the cabin."

"You will be," he said. "Will you try?"

"What is that noise you're making?" asked Cynthia's voice sharply. "Come out!"

John hung up the receiver quickly, pushed back the indicator, and, grabbing a loaf of

bread, followed his companion into the daylight.

"I heard you talking to somebody. Who
was it?" asked Cynthia Dorban.

"I was talking to my favourite squab,"
said John coolly. "Don't you think Mr.
Stamford Mills has a pleasant voice?"

"What were you doing in that pantry?"
asked Cynthia suspiciously, and just then her
husband passed and she called him.

"You were a fool to let them out, anyway," was all the sympathy she had, after
her prisoners had been locked again in their
cabin. "You could have easily brought them
the food they wanted, or let Hollin take it.
And, Cynthia, that girl must be allowed on
deck; I can't have her locked up in a cabin
all the time."

"You can't, can't you?" sneered the
woman. "And may I ask if it's any worse
for her than it was for us?"

He was filling his cigarette-case from the
stock that he had found in the captain's

cabin. He closed the case with a snap, put it carefully into his pocket, and then replied to his wife.

"Anything might happen in the next twenty-four hours, Cynthia, and I ask you to help me that nothing *does* occur for which I shall be sorry."

She went pale in spite of her undoubted courage. There were unsuspected deeps to Slico's character that she had only dimly sensed.

"I have no desire to injure this girl," he went on; "but if I had, then obviously, my dear Cynthia, you would be very much in the way. I suppose you realize that?"

She nodded. She was shaking in every limb; it seemed to her that she had suddenly come into the presence of an evil in the man which she had never, in her most uncharitable moments, imagined. And his next words confirmed that suspicion.

"When you took this girl out into the bay to finish her, I let you go because I had made up my mind that the sweep should be a clean one. Had you come back and told me that she was dead, you would not have lived until the morning. Will you please remember that, Cynthia?"

His silky voice held a menace which struck terror to her soul.

"You wouldn't do that!" she gasped. "I only did it for your sake."

He went out of the cabin smiling, and she dropped heavily to the settee with the terror of death in her heart.

"You have the run of the ship, Miss Pitt," said Arthur Dorban courteously, "though, of course, you will not communicate with any of the people I have very regretfully placed under lock and key. I am sure you do not know what you have been doing, or you would never have assisted these scoundrels in their plans to escape justice."

He stood before the door and made no attempt to enter the cabin, and his attitude was both polite and deferential.

"I promise you that you shall not be interfered with or made uncomfortable, either by myself or by any person who is acting with me—any person," he emphasized.

She nodded her thanks, and he left her.

She strode up and down the deck, trying to regain some of her calm, and she was successful to the extent that when she saw

Hollin sitting on the top of the steps, a rifle across his knee and an even more formidable armoury about his waist, she spoke to him, much to his surprise.

"You're all right, missie," he said reassuringly, for Mr. Hollin was something of a cavalier, even in his sober moments. "I'll see that nobody hurts you."

"Do you know where we are going?"

"Haven't the slightest idea," he replied. "The governor says he's going into a Spanish port, and he's making everything easy for me. Anyway, it'll be thousands of pounds in my pocket."

She thought it would be unwise to question him as to the nature of the promise which Arthur Dorban had evidently made to the man, and strolled forward again, stopping by the red ventilator to lean over the rail. She could see the porthole of Bobby's cabin, and, her heart beating wildly, she went back to her cabin to search for the means to help the man she had promised to marry. In one of the drawers of her desk was a ball of thin string, and from this she cut off a dozen yards and made a slip-knot at one end. She had already made up her mind what she would do. The revolver on Hollin's right hip was nearest this side of the ship, and again she made her way to the man, and this time pulled up a stool so that she sat by his side and a little above him. He looked up and grinned.

"I'm on duty here," he boasted. "The crew live down below." He pointed to the well, where two or three unhappy-looking men were smoking and scowling up at their watcher. "If they get fresh I know how to deal with 'em."

"I suppose so," she faltered, and he misunderstood her agitation.

"Mind you, I wouldn't shoot unless they provoked me. I am a kind-hearted man myself—anybody can make a fool of me"—he leered up at her—"especially wimmin!"

As he turned his head to take a smirking

survey of the well, she made her attempt, and it was successful. Her heart almost stopped beating; she could scarcely breathe; but the pistol came out of the holster, and he did not seem to notice the loss—due probably to the fact that the end of the holster was resting on the deck where he sat.

Presently she got up with an excuse and strolled back along the deck, her knees giving beneath her. With trembling fingers she fastened the end of the string about the butt, and opposite the red ventilator she dropped it gingerly over the side until the pistol swayed before the open porthole. She had to wait, it seemed, almost an eternity before a hand came out, gripped the weapon and drew it in, and she almost fainted with the relief. Gripping the rail to steady herself, she turned, to walk back unconcernedly to where Mr. Hollin was sitting.

He looked round after her, but fortunately had seen nothing suspicious in her action.

"You're feeling a bit sea-sick, ain't you?"

he asked, with the pride of one for whom the
sea had no terrors. "You're looking as white
as death, young lady. Better sit down."

"I think I will," she said.

"Now, you take my advice," said Mr.
Hollin, wagging a solemn and grimy finger
at her, "have nothing to do with this John.
He's a crook and couldn't go straight. He'd
'shop' his best pal. That's what he was
going to do with me—put me adrift in an
open boat, after promising me that he'd take
me to South America and settle me for life.
What do you think of a man like that?"

"I'm sure he would do nothing of the
sort," said Pen.

"Oh, wouldn't he?" said Mr. Hollin sarcastically. "That shows what you know about
it! I can only tell you—— Hullo!" His
hand had dropped upon the empty holster
at his side, and he sprang up. "Now, no
tricks, miss. Where's that gun?"

"Gun?" she said, with an heroic attempt
at surprise.

"I swear I put it in."

He looked at her darkly. It was so obvious that there was no way by which she could conceal a weapon of that size, that he turned to search the deck.

"I'll swear I shoved it into the holder, but perhaps I made a mistake."

"Have you lost something?" she asked innocently, and at that moment a shot rang out, followed by a second and a third, and Hollin dashed frantically for the companionway.

Arthur Dorban and his wife were discussing the course they should follow when they reached Cadiz, when there came to them the sound of a shivering crash. It was the noise of heavy feet kicking at a door, and the noise was easily located.

"If you fellows don't keep quiet, I'll have you tied hand and foot," he threatened from outside the door, and then jumped aside hastily as one of the panels splintered and the door flew open.

He fired from his hip, but the two shots rang out almost at once. He went down to the deck limply.

It was Cynthia who fired the third shot, but her hand was shaking so that the bullet went wide, and in another second John had her by her shoulder and jerked her into Bobby's disengaged arm.

"Into the cabin with her," said John.

They hustled the woman back to the cabin she had left. John found the key of the handcuffs laid out on Mrs. Dorban's dressing-table, together with spare boxes of ammunition, and in an instant he was free, only in time to meet the bull rush of Hollin as he came blundering along the alley-way. Mr. Hollin, a philosopher, accepted the situation and was relieved of his armament.

"Where is Dorban?" asked Bobby. The alley-way was empty.

"I'm going to look for him. Take charge of these people, Bobby."

John stopped only to open the cabins

where the captain and Orford were imprisoned, and then ran up to the deck. Arthur Dorban was nowhere in sight; nor was he on the boat-deck, and save for the two quartermasters who were navigating the yacht, the bridge was empty. Right aft between the two funnels was a small wooden superstructure where the wireless man had his headquarters, and instinctively John made for this spot. Dorban was there; he limped out as John came to the door.

"You're too late, my friend," he said, with that twisted smile of his. "I have induced your operator to send a message which will have uncomfortable results for you."

John pushed him aside and went into the little cubby-hut.

"It's gone out, sir," said the operator. "He threatened to kill me if I didn't send it."

"What have you sent?" asked John quickly.

"I told the warship that you were on board."

"The warship?" said John. "Where?"

He ran out of the hut and, shading his eyes, followed the operator's outstretched finger. Blended in the grey of a heavy cloud that lay upon the horizon, he made out the outlines of a man-o'-war.

"She's talking now, sir," said the operator, and put the receiver to his ears.

"What does she say?" asked John.

"She says : 'Turn hard a-port, and stop your engines a mile from me. I am coming aboard.'"

"Oh, she is, is she?" said John.

The captain was standing by the wheel when he reached the bridge, and out of the corner of his eye he caught a glimpse of Dorban being escorted down the narrow gangway by two seamen. In a few words he explained the situation.

"We shall have to run for it," said the captain. "She's one of the *Myanthic* class, and she hasn't the speed to overtake us."

He gave a brief order, and the vessel

heeled over as she went to starboard, making a complete turn and going back on her own tracks. They had gone half a mile when the wireless operator came with a slip of paper, which he handed to the captain. The old man adjusted his glasses, read and grunted.

"They say if we do not stop they will open fire on us."

He took up a rubber speaking-tube from the navigating desk.

"Hit her up, Mackenzie," he growled. "You've got to beat records!"

He had scarcely spoken when a puff of smoke moved lazily from the side of the warship; they heard the dull boom of a gun, and saw a fountain of water splash up where the shell had struck. Again came the wisp of smoke and again the boom, but this time the shell fell nearer.

"We're too big a target," said the captain. "A point to port, quartermaster. We'll give her our stern to aim at."

Two guns were now in action. John saw the flash of their explosions and heard the shriek of the shells. A third fell, then a fourth, that carried away a stay of the main-mast, but did no further damage. No other shot came as near, and soon the war vessel ceased firing. There followed a hasty council of war in the main saloon. Penelope saw them through an open skylight, grouped about a table covered with charts.

"This is where organization comes in," said Mr. Orford, cheerful for the first time in many days. "Here's the point, Captain." He made a small pencil mark on one of the charts. "I've got an oilship there, waiting to refuel us. She had to leave for Penzance with only a fortnight's supply. And I've charted this oiler to wait for us at this spot. She's an American."

"I'm not worried about juice," said the captain. "We've got enough to carry us for another ten days. What's worrying me is the fact that in twenty-four hours these waters will be alive with fast destroyers looking for us. They've an aeroplane-carrier at Gibraltar, and she'll be out. I don't see how we can miss being caught."

"Let 'em catch us," said Orford genially. "The only evidence against you, Captain, is the evidence of these people we have on board."

"And the presence of Mr.—John," corrected the captain. "*And* the young lady."

"Quite so," nodded Orford. "But suppose, when they overhaul you, we are not on board."

"Where can you be?" asked the captain. "We can't take *Polyantha* back to the Spanish coast."

"We'll transfer to the oilship. She's going back to Boston, Massachusetts. And nobody will be any the wiser. The captain is a friend of mine and I can keep the crew quiet."

The skipper bit his lip thoughtfully.

"If she's there," he said.

"She'll be there," said Mr. Orford, with a touch of asperity in his voice. "I have arranged it."

John went up on deck to explain the position to the girl.

"I'm afraid we can't give you such comfortable accommodation on the oilship," he said. "But at least you will have a definite destination. We are going to Boston, and we shall reach there in ten days, and all your troubles will be at an end; and, by Jove, you'll get back to Canada after all!"

She smiled, a little sadly.

"I didn't expect to get back to Canada that way," she said. "But so long as we get anywhere——"

She was piqued, and she couldn't quite understand why, until she remembered that what had hurt her was his apparent acceptance of her desire to go back to Canada, and that he had not again made any mention of the fantastic marriage which Orford had planned. It was fantastical, but she had agreed, and she deserved a little consideration.

"I am being rather sorry for myself," she confessed, and could have bitten her tongue that she had made such a confession.

Happily he did not seem to follow her train of thoughts.

"I shall be perfectly happy on an oilboat," she said. "Please don't trouble about me. Though I am really getting fond of the *Polyantha*, and am sorry to leave her."

"In spite of the exciting and mysterious time you're having?" he smiled, and she nodded.

So perfect was Mr. Orford's organization that at two o'clock in the morning they picked up the oilship, and the providential calmness of the sea made it possible to get alongside her.

IT was raining when Penelope climbed up a greasy monkey-ladder on to the untidy steel deck of the oilship. Mr. Orford in some miraculous fashion had already made that perilous climb; and so excellent were his gifts for organization that, when they reached the officers' quarters, which were aft, they found accommodation of unexpected comfort awaiting the party. The two ships parted company at dawn, and Penelope, through the litter of coiled ropes and rusty anchor chains, stood watching the stately lines of the *Polyantha* growing fainter and fainter in a misty drizzle.

The oilship lacked many of the qualities which had distinguished *Polyantha*. She rolled tremendously and she pitched upon the slightest provocation. Mrs. Dorban, who was susceptible to these movements, and to whom the overpowering smell of oil added a new horror to the sea, went to her bunk and remained there the whole of the next day.

Penelope's cabin was a small one, and she had some difficulty in stowing away even her few possessions. The cabin drawers were filled with the belongings of its first occupant, but she made herself comfortable however, and though she was not looking forward to the end of the adventure, for reasons which she could not quite explain to herself, she was anticipating with some eagerness the end of this particular period.

She saw John on deck next morning, and he gave her a piece of news which surprised her.

"I don't think you've said good-bye to the *Polyantha*," he said. "Orford has just told me that he has made another rendez-vous, and if *Polyantha* comes through the search to which she will undoubtedly be sub-jected when she is stopped by the first warship, she will meet us north of Madeira, and the chances are that our voyage will be continued under less smelly conditions."

"What are you going to do with the Dorbans?" she asked. "And Hollin?"

"I shall have to take Hollin on, as I promised. As to the Dorbans——" He shook his head. "They are a difficulty, but I think money will buy them—money and a promise, which I have half-made."

"What is that?" she asked curiously.

He looked away from her for some time, and then:

"I have promised that I will not marry, on condition that they do not betray me. I have never despised myself so much as I have since that promise was made." His eyes came back to hers.

"Why?" she asked.

"Because I love you," he said, "and I'm cutting myself away from the one happiness of all happinesses that I most desire. You must think I'm rather a cad, Penelope, and

I suppose I am," he said. "I did want to marry you for—for diplomatic reasons. But I realized, of course, that, though you were so gracious as to accept Orford's suggestion, you did so from no feeling of love for me. How could you? You have only known me for a few days, and even now you do not know the worst about me."

"I think I do," she said.

He shook his head.

"You're running away from somebody. You have committed"—she hesitated in search of a word—"a crime?"

"No, I have committed no crime. I have been accused—but what is the good?"

She looked after him as he walked away, and there was a hollow, empty feeling in her heart, as though something which was part of her had gone out.

That afternoon they passed two questing torpedo-boat destroyers, who asked them if they had seen *Polyantha*, and received an untruthful "No." Toward evening, a code wireless message came through to the oilship, one which had been prearranged by Mr. Orford.

"She is being stopped and searched," explained Mr. Orford at dinner that night."

"Poor Bobby!" murmured the girl. They had left Bobby to play the part of plutocratic owner.

"Bobby is a natural liar," said John calmly. "He has a gift of prevarication which would make his fortune if he ever turned to literature. How is your wife, Dorban?"

Mr. Arthur Dorban smiled cryptically, but made no reply.

Later in the evening they were sitting on the after-deck when the captain of the *Ezra Salt* came aft. John and Mr. Orford were smoking, the girl was huddled up in a deck-chair, for the motion of the ship had grown a trifle unpleasant, and Arthur Dorban was pacing unsteadily the steel deck.

"I've just picked up an S.O.S. message,

Mr. Orford," the captain said, "that the *Pealego* has struck some submerged wreckage and is sinking."

"What is the *Pealego?*"

"She's a passenger-boat that works the Vigo-Funchal route. A crazy ship; I've seen her a dozen times in these waters. I have altered my course and am standing for her. She went down about twenty miles from where we were when we had the message, and we ought to fall in with her boats very soon."

In these simple, unemotional words did he tell of one of the tragedies of the sea.

Three hours passed when they caught sight of a flare burning ahead, and distinguished two boats rowing in company.

"This is mighty awkward for us," said Mr. Orford, shaking his head. "We shall have to put these people ashore somewhere, and land I did not wish to tread until I stepped out on to the quay in Boston, Massachusetts."

The crew of the *Ezra Salt* were rigging a branch-lamp over the gangway, which had been lowered, and they gathered, a little, interested group, to watch the rescued party brought on board. Two hysterical women wrapped in sailors' coats came first, and were hurried below; then came a bedraggled old man; and, following him, a tall, soldierlike person, who stepped smartly on to the deck and looked round. And the first person he saw was John. John did not move a muscle as the man came up to him.

"My name is Inspector Spinner," he said, "and I think I know you."

"It is very likely," said John coolly.

"You are the Earl of Rivertor, a convict undergoing a sentence of twenty years' penal servitude for forgery, and this man is James Hollin, a convict undergoing five years for burglary. You are both fugitives from justice, having escaped from Dartmoor Prison on the morning of the fourteenth instant."

" I can corroborate that statement," said a voice, and Arthur Dorban pushed his way through the group. " My name is Arthur Dorban and this man is my cousin."

To the girl's astonishment John turned upon his enemy with a beatific smile.

" That lets me out of my promise, Arthur," he said.

*   *   *   *   *

To Penelope Pitt the night was one long ugly dream. She was so incapable of separating reality from phantasm, that at one moment she was seriously concerned for her reason. John was the Earl of Rivertor! He was an escaped convict! The thing was so incredible, so sheerly fantastical, that a dozen times in the night she sat up in her narrow bunk and switched on the light, to convince herself that she was awake and not the victim of a nightmare.

What had happened to the portly Mr. Orford she did not know. Nor could she summon sufficient mental energy to speculate upon her own fate, and in how so far she was implicated.

When the early watch was busy with its hosepipes and holystone, and before the sun had tipped the horizon, she had dressed and gone to the deck. If she was interested in the welfare of Mr. Orford, her apprehensions would have been set at rest instantly, for, muffled to his many chins in a heavy coat, his legs covered by numerous rugs and wrappings, she found him in the one comfortable chair which the *Ezra Salt* possessed.

He was wide awake and brooding and, although she anticipated something of reproach in his manner, since she felt indirectly responsible for the disastrous ending to all his fine schemes, he met her with a smile which was almost paternal.

" No, I haven't been to bed, and I haven't been to sleep."

" Please don't get up," she begged hastily, as he made an attempt to disentangle himself from his coverings. " I can sit here." She pulled up a stool to his side. "Mr. Orford, what does it all mean?"

"What does it all mean?" he repeated, with strange and, to her, comforting deliberation. "Why, it means that six months' hard work, half a million dollars, and the best organized get-away that the world has ever known, has gone——!" He snapped his fingers expressively.

"Won't you please tell me the whole story?" she begged, and he nodded.

"I guess there's no reason why you shouldn't know," he said. "Hi!" He beckoned a sailor. "Son, will you go down to the cook's galley and bring up some coffee."

The lank youth he had called disappeared with a grunt.

"John is the Earl of Rivertor," said Xenocrates without preliminary, "though he wasn't the Earl of Rivertor when he was sent down for twenty years. And, what is more, he had not the slightest idea that he stood in the line for the title. He is a rich man; so is Mr. Stamford Mills, his friend. They were art students together in Paris, and since Lord Rivertor has been sent to prison that young man has been working like one small slave to get him out.

"I have been responsible for a whole range of organizations in my time," he went on reminiscently. "I've organized everything from Balkan wars to oil flotations. But I've never organized a man out of prison with such perfect ingenuity——" He stopped and shook his head. "This trouble began when Hollin's cap flew off, because an English convict has a number, and that number is embroidered on his cap."

"Won't you begin at the beginning?" she asked. "Why was Lord Rivertor sent to prison? What crime did he commit?"

"He committed none; of that I am convinced," said Mr. Orford emphatically. "Now see here, Miss Pitt. It's been my experience that every man that goes to prison is innocent. The gaols are filled with victims of malignant fate and vicious conspiracy. I've got so that when I meet a man who has been in gaol, I expect a declaration of innocence, and I should be disappointed if I didn't get it. It is always the other fellow who did it, or there has been a frame-up; or sometimes it is an unpleasant coincidence that put them behind the bars. So, when I heard that this Lord Rivertor was the victim of a vile conspiracy, why, I naturally felt that I was meeting a normal case of the law's grinding injustice. But he *is* innocent."

Mr. Orford emphasized this word with a jerk of his fat forefinger in Penelope's direction.

"And it *was* a frame-up. He was an artist, the third cousin, or the fourth—the Lord knows which—of the old Earl of Rivertor, who had three sons, all of whom died in one week of influenza. That sounds like one of the stories we used to read when we were young," he chuckled; "though usually it was a yachting accident that removed the lawful heir and gave to the poor but honest farmhand the ancestral estates. But these men died naturally; I've had a very careful investigation into that, because I more than suspected that Dorban assisted Nature in her hideous work of dissolution.

"John Rivertor knew nothing about this. He was an artist—not a struggling artist; he had a small income—and he specialized in etchings. Maybe he was a good etcher, maybe he wasn't; I don't profess to understand very much about art. Now, it appears, from what was subsequently revealed at the trial, that John was in the habit of frequenting a restaurant in the West End of London. And the proprietor of the restaurant had on several occasions found amongst his cash forged five-pound Bank of England notes. He couldn't trace the customer from whom the notes had been received, but suspicion fell on John. How suspicion may be engendered is clearly understandable to the psychologist, and I have at the back of my mind a fairly good idea as to the identity of the gentleman who set rumour moving. I guess, too, that he sent a few of the notes into circulation.

" John was not a rich man, but, as I said before, he was fairly comfortable, and he practically lived for his work. One day there arrived in his studio a man who said that he was buying etchings for an American millionaire. John had never seen him before —has never seen him since. He chose a couple of prints and offered a very large sum, much to John's surprise. In fact, he asked the man to take these pictures for less than he'd offered, but the fellow insisted on paying the sum he had mentioned. He paid in banknotes. The first half-dozen were genuine; the others were clever, but not too clever, forgeries. He took the pictures away with him, and John accompanied him to the railway station at his visitor's request. The visitor gave the name of 'Smith.' He said he was going on to Brussels, and there was nothing very remarkable about the transaction except the large price he had paid for the etchings. He kept John an unconscionable time at the railway depôt, and at last they parted, and John went on to dine at his favourite restaurant. He was not particularly uncomfortable at having so much money in his possession, and he did not give that fact two minutes' thought.

"He had finished his dinner, and was leaving the restaurant, when he was arrested by two detectives, taken to a police station and searched. The forged notes were found upon him; and though he explained how they came to be there, his explanation was not accepted. The police immediately sent to his studio and made a search. The studio consisted of a large room where he worked, two small bedrooms, a lumber-room, and a kitchenette. In the lumber-room, which was locked, the police discovered a complete counterfeiting outfit—presses, plates, stacks of notes apparently new from the press, acid-baths, etching tools, and what not. The evidence was overpowering; and although experts in forgery gave their opinion that these notes were of German make and the work of crude forgers who turned these things out by the hundreds of thousands, John was found guilty, and since it appeared that the police had captured a very dangerous criminal and a master-forger, the heaviest sentence that the law of England allowed was passed upon him—twenty years' penal servitude.

"What is amazing to me"—he frowned at the girl—"is that you did not know all this, because the English and the New York newspapers were filled with the account, not only of the trial, but of the subsequent discovery that the man who had been sentenced to what was tantamount to a life imprisonment, was the Earl of Rivertor, a peer, who had inherited, not only the title, but nearly ten million dollars."

She had listened, speechless with amazement, as the story was unfolded. Now she shook her head.

"It did not get as far as Edmonton, or, if it did, I have not read this in the news," she said. "When did this happen?"

"A year and seventeen days ago," replied Mr. Orford correctly. And then she understood.

"I was away on a farm for six months, and saw no newspapers," she said. "Of course, that would be the reason; the Edmonton newspapers must have published accounts, because Lord Rivertor has a big ranch in the neighbourhood."

"Maybe he has," said Mr. Orford. "Anyway, John went to prison. Now, Mr. Mills, who is a very great friend of Lord Rivertor's, set himself the task of unearthing the mystery of John's conviction. He was perfectly satisfied that the story John had told at the trial was true. His first object was to find the relatives who would benefit by this man being detached from the world; and he very soon unearthed Slico. Slico is Lord Rivertor's first cousin and the next in line for the title."

"But Lord Rivertor is a very young man," interrupted Penelope. "Twenty years is not a long time. How could they be sure that the title and the money would come to the Dorbans?"

"They left nothing to chance," said Xenocrates grimly. "A month after he had been transferred to Dartmoor, he was taken violently ill. Meals are served by convict orderlies. They're not exactly 'trusties,' as we understand 'trusties,' but have certain privileges and easy jobs because they have behaved themselves in prison. There is no doubt that in some manner the food that was given to John was poisoned. The prison doctor discovered arsenic, and there was an inquiry on the subject. Two months later,

the rifle which one of the warders carried
went off 'accidentally,' and the bullet passed
within a millimetre of Lord Rivertor's head.
Bobby, who is a born sleuth, discovered that
the warder was a man who had been repri-
manded for various offences and was practically under suspension. He discovered,
too, that this official was in communication
with the Dorbans, and had made several
visits to the Stone House at Borcombe.
After each visit his banking account had been
considerably augmented. Why, do you
imagine, did Arthur Dorban live at Borcombe, shut away from the world?"

"I thought he was in retirement——"

"Because of his past? Not a bit of it,"
said Mr. Orford with a slow smile. "Dorban was at Borcombe because it was near to
Dartmoor, because he could get into communication with his agents in the prison without delay. Why do you think they brought
you from Canada? Because you knew
nothing of the case, because you had no

friends in England—— Gosh, if I had only known!" He slapped his swathed knees impatiently.

"After a third attempt on his life, carried out by a convict, Bobby consulted me. I am willing to admit," said Mr. Orford thoughtfully, "that a very large fee had a great deal to do with my undertaking this commission. Once I had set my mind to it, the rest was easy. We chartered the *Polyantha* for six months from a French nobleman, commissioned it with picked men—the doctor is a distant relative of John's, and the old captain is a maternal uncle—and set out to sea in time for the great attempt. Bobby Mills was in the air service during the war, and he was able to buy an aeroplane from the Disposal Board, and he got an armoured car from the junk store.

"John was a worker in the quarries, and the quarries are outside of the prison. Every morning and afternoon, a party marches out from Princetown Gaol up a country road to the quarry, which isn't a very great distance. John was in No. 6 party, the first to leave the prison. On the morning of the fourteenth, an armoured car came into the little town, driven apparently by a soldier; in reality the driver was our second engineer. He proceeded slowly up the road until he came within sight of the prison, and there he stopped and got down to tinker with the engine. Presently, he saw the party march out, and, jumping on to his seat, he let the car go, at first slowly, and then with increasing speed, until he came abreast of the leading file.

"John was in the fourth file, and he had been carefully primed. I'm not going to tell you by what corrupt method we gave him information of our plans, but he knew. As the car came up to him, he sprang on to the running-board and dived into the steel-plated interior, and the driver increased his speed. Unfortunately, in the leading file was a convict named Hollin, who saw here

an opportunity too good to be lost, and before
the driver could realize what had happened,
he had also jumped into the car and struck
down the warder who attempted to pull him
back."

"Is that what they call 'scragging?'"
asked the girl, a light dawning upon her.

"It's what he calls 'scragging.' It's an
ugly word used by the lower class English,
and means killing—though he didn't kill the
warder, not by any means. The car dashed
on, its steel back taking the bullets which
were fired after it, and came to a quiet part
of the moor, where Bobby was waiting with
his aeroplane. They had to take Hollin;
there was no help for it. If his cap had not
blown off near the coast, they might not have
guessed the direction we took or the method
we employed."

"And the *Polyantha* was waiting?" asked
the girl.

He nodded.

"Yes, she was waiting. Everything went

to schedule. We had had the aeroplane specially buoyed to keep her afloat in the sea, and down she came within a dozen yards of the gangway. We took out John and this brute Hollin, bombed the aeroplane and sank her, and thereafter everything seemed smooth sailing."

"Until I came aboard," she said ruefully.

"Until you came aboard," he agreed. "What's the matter?"

She got up suddenly, white of face.

"The notes!" she gasped. "And the etchings!"

"What do you mean?" he demanded, struggling to his feet.

Incoherently, she told the story of what she had seen—the trunk packed with notes, and the etchings on top—and Mr. Orford heard and groaned.

"If I had only known," he wailed. "Of course, that was it! The notes were the surplus stock they brought over for the frame-up. And the etchings! Oh, hell!"

They stared at one another.

"Those notes are at the bottom of the sea now," said Mr. Orford. "The last bit of evidence!"

"There was a receipt," she said slowly. "I forget the exact wording. It was a receipt signed by Mr. Feltham."

"Yes, yes," he said eagerly, "John Feltham—that was John's family name. What happened?"

"I'm trying to think." She sat down, her face in her hands. The receipt—what had happened to it? She put it on the window-sill, and it blew into the garden, and then she picked it up—that dreadful night when Cynthia Dorban had made her wicked attempt to kill her.

"I put it somewhere. I'm sure I put it somewhere," she said. "I know I didn't throw it away—the sports jacket," she said eagerly. "Do you remember the sports jacket I wore on the *Polyantha?*"

"Where is it?" he asked, in a tone a little above a husky whisper.

"I left it—on the *Polyantha*," she said breathlessly, "hanging in the wardrobe."

Mr. Orford collapsed into his chair.

"And I told the captain to throw overboard anything he found that might betray your presence!" he said hollowly.

THE motion of the ship was steadier. The sea had evidently subsided, when Cynthia Dorban woke, to find her husband gazing gloomily through the open porthole, his elbows upon the casing, his smooth forehead wrinkled in thought. He was fully dressed, she noted.

"Is anything wrong?" she asked quickly.

He did not turn his head toward her.

"No, nothing is wrong. Except that the girl knows."

"The girl knows!" repeated the woman scornfully. "Of course she knows! Who told her? Did you tell her all about it?"

"I haven't spoken to her. But she and Orford have had their heads together on the deck, and I think she has told him."

"What?"

"About the notes and the etchings she found in the trunk."

Cynthia smiled.

"If he wants to find those, he'll have to dive for them," she said.

"I wonder," he said mechanically.

"You wonder? I put them into the water myself."

"They should have been burnt," he said, still addressing the open porthole. "I always said they should have been burnt. But it's too late to trouble about that. Suppose she swears to what she saw? That will make it rather awkward for you and me, Cynthia."

Cynthia got out of her bunk and put on her dressing-gown before she answered.

"You're a fool. I never realized what a weakling you were until we came on this beastly ship—the *Polyantha*, I mean. Suppose she does swear? Her word against a conviction in a court of law? You don't imagine that pardons are signed in England on that kind of evidence, do you?"

"Also," he went on, not answering her question, "Whiplow is on board."

She gaped at him.

"Whiplow here?" she said incredulously.

He nodded.

"He was one of the people we picked up last night. He was in the second boat. Apparently he and Spinner were on their way to Madeira when the *Peleago* struck. Don't ask me why they were going to Madeira, because I don't know. I gathered this from a conversation I heard between Whiplow and the captain of the ship."

"Have you spoken to him?"

He shook his head.

"It is not expedient that I should even know him. I dare say he will not be quite as reticent, but I want to get at him quietly. That is why I was up so early, but the beast isn't an early riser."

She sat down on the side of her bunk to consider the situation.

"I don't see that it makes a great deal of

difference to us whether he's here or isn't here," she said.

He turned and looked at her steadily.

"It makes a whole lot of difference," he said slowly. "And that you will live to discover."

"What do you mean?"

"For a woman so clever, you can be exceedingly dense," said Arthur. "I am going on deck. Shall I send in your breakfast?"

She shivered.

"I see that you still have qualms. I will send you a biscuit and soda-water."

The first person he met on deck was Mr. Orford, and the stout man was bland and almost genial.

"How is your friend this morning?" asked Dorban.

"Haven't seen him," said Mr. Orford. "But I guess he's eaten a better breakfast than you, Dorban. Wonderful thing, a clear conscience."

Arthur smiled.

"How will this affect you? You're in the conspiracy, and I presume that you are virtually under arrest."

"I'm under suspicion," admitted Xenocrates Orford carefully, "but who isn't?"

Arthur chuckled.

"I'm not for one. Why are you in this business at all? You must have spent a lot of money. And you can't say that you've had an overwhelming success, can you?"

"Sir," said Mr. Orford, "the end is not yet. I have sufficient faith in my especial providence to keep me calm in such crises as these."

"You'll need a very special providence to get you out of your present mess," said Arthur.

A blur of smoke on the horizon caught his eye.

"I wonder," he said.

Mr. Orford peered at the smoke, and instinct told him its significance.

"The *Polyantha!*" he gasped, and Dorban laughed aloud.

"I hope it is the *Polyantha*, for I'm tired of this infernal oilship," he said. "I will not mystify you, Mr. Orford. When Spinner arrested my relative last night and searched him, there was found in his pocket a small code-book."

Orford made a clicking noise with his lips, which El Slico altogether misunderstood.

"So we took the liberty of sending a message to the *Polyantha*, asking her to join us at full speed. Fortunately, she was on a parallel course. You see, Mr. Orford," he went on, almost apologetically, "we decided that it would be advisable to catch the whole gang, including Mr. Bobby Mills."

"I see," nodded Orford.

It was at that moment that John appeared, accompanied by his captor. He nodded to Orford, and met his cousin's smile without any evidence of embarrassment.

"Spinner tells me *Polyantha's* coming up hand over fist; well, at least we shall have a comfortable voyage to England." He turned to the detective. "I suppose that it is against the rule for me to have a few words with Mr. Orford?"

Spinner hesitated.

"I don't know that there are any particular rules applying," he said. "You can speak in my presence."

"Thank you." John looked at Dorban, and that imperturbable gentleman walked away with a shrug. "Is Miss Pitt very much alarmed?"

"She is just a little," said Mr. Orford carefully. "John, do you remember whether I told Willit to make a very careful search of Miss Pitt's cabin? I'm so worried that I can't recall."

John nodded.

"I remember you giving those instructions. Why?"

Mr. Orford licked his dry lips.

"I won't tell you now," he said. "Maybe I'll never tell you." Then, to the detective: "Do you remember the trial?"

Spinner nodded.

"I arrested Lord Rivertor," he said.

"You remember the defence?"

The inspector smiled faintly.

"There wasn't much of a defence, was there, Mr. Orford? It was suggested that the case was what you call in America a 'frame-up,' that the machinery and notes had been planted whilst Feltham was out."

"But you remember the story he told that he had sold two etchings to a stranger whom he never saw again, and that the money found in his possession was the proceeds of that sale?"

The inspector nodded.

"Suppose"—Orford's voice was lowered to little more than a whisper—"suppose I find the receipt? Suppose Lord Rivertor identifies the man who bought the pictures? And on top of that, we give you the evidence of one who saw the etchings in Dorban's possession."

Spinner fingered his chin and frowned.

Mr. Orford's earnestness was very convincing.

"It would make a difference, of course," he said. "The Secretary of State would reopen the question, and if it was proved——" He shook his head. "But I don't think you've much chance of getting proof. Suppose you produced the receipt—it might be faked!"

"I'm going to take you into my confidence," said Orford, with his eye upon Arthur, leaning over the rail. "Here is a new angle to the story."

He spoke quickly, and John listened in amazement as he revealed all that Penelope Pitt had told. And then, in the midst of his narrative, a man walked on to the deck and dropped his hand familiarly upon Arthur Dorban's shoulder. They could only see the back of him, but presently his head turned, and then:

"Who is that man?" hissed Orford fiercely.

John turned, then, with a cry, leapt at the stranger, and before he could escape had caught him by the throat.

"You know me?" he demanded.

Whiplow, struggling in his grip, was ashen pale.

"I don't know you!" he shouted. "And I've never seen you. Let go!"

John released his hold.

"This is the man who came to my studio and bought two etchings from me and paid me in banknotes," he said. "This is the man my friends have been trying to find, and whom I have never seen since that day."

"You're mad!" breathed Whiplow, adjusting his disordered jacket. "You're a stranger to me!"

And then the detective took John by the arm and led him away.

"It's possible that you're right, Lord Rivertor," he said; "and if you're acting, it's the best bit of acting I've seen for years. What do you say the man's name is?"

"Whiplow," said John, breathing heavily. "He's a friend of Dorban's——"

"Whiplow?" muttered the detective. "I seem to know that name. Just give me a little time to think, will you?"

There was little time for quiet meditation, for the *Polyantha* was now within a few miles of the oilship, whose engines had rung to stop.

Half an hour later, Spinner left for the *Polyantha* alone, and it was two hours before he returned. On his arm was a yellow sports coat, and Penelope, watching the approaching boat, felt her heart leap within her. Was the paper there? She looked round for Mr. Orford, but he was not in sight. Neither was Whiplow. Arthur Dorban and his wife stood by the gangway, puzzled, a little worried, the girl thought.

"Why didn't he take us off at once?" asked Cynthia irritably. "Why did he go on to the yacht——"

"Ask him," said Slico laconically as the detective appeared.

"Where is your friend?" he asked, and there was something in his voice which Dorban, being a man sensitive to atmosphere, did not like.

"Whiplow? He's below, I expect. He's not a friend of mine, by the way, Inspector."

Without a word Spinner went in search of his man.

* * * * *

Behind the locked door of Mr. Orford's cabin that gentleman spoke his final word.

"I'm not very well acquainted with the laws of England, Whiplow, but I guess that there is such a thing as State evidence. And anyway, what would be a few years of imprisonment to a man like you, if you knew that you were coming out to a whole heap of money?"

"How do I know that you'd pay?" asked Mr. Whiplow miserably.

"You'd have to trust me," said Mr. Orford. "And I'm not asking you much,
Whiplow, for I have sufficient evidence to
hang you. Now, boy"—he laid his hand on
the other's shoulder with a solemnity which
was peculiarly his own—"before the bulls
start to gore you, will you get in right?"

Whiplow stared down at the floor sulkily.

It was the last throw of James Xenocrates
Orford, the last coin on the board of chance,
but this the other did not know.

"Spinner is wise to you. We've got the
receipt you signed, the phoney notes are in
the hands of the police, and Dorban will
leave this ship in irons. Now, are you going
with him to share the life sentence he'll get,
or are you going to behave sensibly?"

"I've never squealed in my life," said
Whiplow nervously; "and there's no
evidence against me. How do I know that
you'll pay?" he asked again.

Mr. Orford had almost convinced his unwilling guest when there came a tap at the

door. With a calm which was almost awful, remembering the circumstances, he pulled back the bolt and opened the door, to meet Inspector Spinner, and in Mr. Spinner's hand was a piece of paper.

"I think this is what you want," he said. But before Orford could reply, Whiplow had pushed him aside and was staring at the crumpled receipt.

"King's evidence!" he said incoherently, and James Xenocrates Orford heaved a deep sigh and sat down heavily on the tiny settee.

Chapter the Last

MR. JAMES XENOCRATES ORFORD sat at his desk overlooking the Park. The afternoon was cool, but all the windows were open, for on this afternoon the band played and the zoomph, zoomph of the euphonium came at intervals to his appreciative ear.

He had spent a somewhat hectic month, and the tenth day of the *Polyantha* had been exceptionally emotional, for he had organized a wedding that had turned simple Penelope Pitt into Penelope, Countess of Rivertor. It had been a very simple wedding. The altar was a soap-box covered with an ensign, and Captain Willit had lost the place in the Prayer-Book some seven times, and had mistakenly churched, buried, and ordained two young people into the priesthood.

And he had given evidence before in-

318

numerable judges and magistrates and under-secretaries of State. And at last he had organized a honeymoon trip with care and precision.

He sat listening to the band, and did not notice his secretary until that unprepossessing lady stood at his side.

"Eh? Mr. Mills? Show him right here. 'Lo, Bobby!"

Bobby gripped the stout Mr. Orford's hand.

"Settling? Why, yes, I suppose so. Use that blotter, Bobby. Thank you."

He examined the cheque thoughtfully.

"Yeh; that's mighty generous. But Rivertor came best out of it. What a girl!"

He sighed heavily, gasped despairingly at the cheque, and then:

"There are times when I fret sump'n fierce—about being fat—and old——".

Nevertheless he smiled when he put the cheque into his pocket.

THE END